Paul Collis is a Barkindji man, born in Bourke in far western NSW on the Darling River. Paul worked in Newcastle for much of his young adult life in the areas of teaching and in Aboriginal community development positions. He has taught Aboriginal Studies to Indigenous inmates at the Worimi and Mount Penang juvenile detention centres and in Cessnock and Maitland prisons. Paul has a Bachelor of Arts degree and a doctorate in communications. He lives in Canberra and works as a creative writing academic at the University of Canberra. *Dancing Home* is his first novel and won the David Unaipon Award in 2016.

First Nations Classics

DANCING HOME

PAUL COLLIS

UQP

First published 2017 by University of Queensland Press
PO Box 6042, St Lucia, Queensland 4067 Australia
This First Nations Classics edition published 2025

University of Queensland Press (UQP) acknowledges the Traditional Owners and their custodianship of the lands on which UQP operates. We pay our respects to their Ancestors and their descendants, who continue cultural and spiritual connections to Country. We recognise their valuable contributions to Australian and global society.

uqp.com.au
reception@uqp.com.au

Cover design by Jenna Lee
Typeset in 11.5/16 pt Bembo Std Regular by Post Pre-press Group, Brisbane
Printed in Australia by McPherson's Printing Group

Queensland Government

University of Queensland Press is supported by the Queensland Government through Arts Queensland.

Australian Government

Creative Australia

First Nations Classics are assisted by the Australian Government through Creative Australia, its principal arts investment and advisory body.

This project is supported by the Copyright Agency's Cultural Fund.

COPYRIGHTAGENCY CULTURAL FUND

A catalogue record for this book is available from the National Library of Australia.

ISBN 978 0 7022 6918 9 (pbk)
ISBN 978 0 7022 7085 7 (epdf)
ISBN 978 0 7022 7086 4 (epub)

University of Queensland Press uses papers that are natural, renewable and recyclable products made from wood grown in well-managed forests and other controlled sources. The logging and manufacturing processes conform to the environmental regulations of the country of origin.

FSC www.fsc.org MIX Paper | Supporting responsible forestry FSC® C001695

For my brother Glenn, champion, and …

for all the Invisible people who live in the shadows.

Introduction
by Samuel Wagan Watson

When I first met the author of this brilliant book, I'm not quite sure what I was thinking. Perhaps I'd laid dangerous foundations. A rubber stamp should have embossed the words: *WARNING! HANDLE WITH CARE.* Supposing Paul Collis did not need the encouragement, his contemplation of a narrative was already in gear. His training wheels firmly grafted – a Black man living and studying in the nation's capital of Canberra – he related to struggle. But once in receipt of a doctorate he realised the true value of a golden goose!

In finding a platform for this new genre of Koori-noir, Collis redefines what it means to be a Unaipon acolyte. Winner of the David Unaipon Award in 2016, *Dancing Home* is the ideal project through which an emerging wordsmith has showcased his talent, artistry, skill and imagination. The death and taxes paradigm secures Collis's place among the UQP Black writers' collective and proves him worthy of a seat at the table. Prolific has been this writer's foxtrot of choice; I constantly receive emails from him flowing with verse.

Whether or not he is collecting these pieces for a future manuscript is yet to be known. His season of inspiration is upon us – in bloom.

There is a harsh variable in Collis's creation of Koori-noir: the paradox of the Aboriginal condition. Collis is capable of tearing a leaf from Oppenheimer's pages: '*NOW I AM BECOME DEATH, DESTROYER OF WORLDS!*' During the completion of *Dancing Home*, a malaise could have easily pushed him into deleting the manuscript. Much Sorry Business was surrounding him. Gallantly, he found a way to honour his loved ones on Country. I can picture him using his time on the back roads. Cassette deck. Endless dust off the bitumen shoulder. Exorcising spectres of Blackie and Rips in the rear-view mirror.

In the 1990s, individuals like Quentin Tarantino injected film with travesties of 'Blaxploitation' and 'Mexican-isms' in a commercial form of such wide reach and influence that very few of us questioned or acknowledged the cultural appropriation taking place. My wish is this: Koori-noir remains positive in its pure medium. That living characters like Blackie and Rips deserve the same opportunities as their post-colonial counterparts, minus the self-destruction.

A convention of the David Unaipon Award is time for research and development of one's manuscript. I'm still really hopeful that now is an optimal time for Koori-noir to sprout taproots and grow into an academic apparatus that is widely studied by First Nations writers and audiences. On the east coast of this continent, a majority of Indigenous Australians can relate or connect to 'Koori time' and can taste the authentic richness of Collis's textured language and Black humour. I have hope for Koori-noir. As with Alan Duff's *Once Were Warriors* – with its rendering of a colonial Aotearoa and the juxtapositions of Māori struggles – the raw language illustrated in Duff's pages is not far from the war cry that linguistically erupts from Collis's simple and pure reclamation of 'urban rhythms' on the page.

In a scene from *Dancing Home*, Blackie and Rips scan the street over with a sweep of their eyes – searching for what is and isn't there – 'looking for people in blue'. Without speaking, they exchange glances, satisfied that the street is clean of copper dogs. They walk like the street is all theirs, 'feeling strong, fearless, and frightfully fucken lucky'. They cross the road and into the pub where 'the smell of stinking sweat and dirty people' hits like a punch in the face. Blackie notices some young guys huddled in a corner 'with their pants hanging down around their arses, wearing hoodies, trying to look dark and dangerous'.

This is a prime example of the author's dab hand at *noir.* The colour palette suitable for cradling predatory desires. The backdrop is harsh but negotiable when the hunted protagonists answer the base urge to hunt. And appearing among the yin and yang of shadows is a young Koori mother 'sat breastfeeding her baby', offering the reader a glimpse of vulnerability, just doing what is natural in a setting that could become vicious at any moment.

At this point in time, all Indigenous voices should be anxious about the edge of tomorrow, especially concerning how artificial intelligence may determine which tongues will witness extinction. Soothing to many of us is that Collis breathes real life into his shadows, and thus these shadows make flesh. Thank goodness there is nothing 'Dickensian' in his gait except a working-class hero. I have witnessed firsthand the artist, and destroyer, receive much respect from his creative writing students and academic peers alike. All is good in Dr Paul Collis's realm, where *Dancing Home* has spawned inspiration for the Unaipon legacy to live on.

Dear Reader,

I invite you to be a player, to be 'active' in the novel *Dancing Home*. Take sides. Be involved in the ideas I've written into this book. Think about poverty, power, privilege, suicide and Aboriginal deaths in custody.

Paul Collis
July 2017

PART I

1

Travel Plans

'Slept with both of 'em!' Carlos boasted. 'And the Antz Pantz chick, you know her? On that ad? Useda go out with her too. Taught her to play pool.'

Blackie was sick of listening to the big-noting bullshit that Carlos had been spilling – for the best part of two hours – since they left the windy coast. The wild city of Sydney was beginning to seem distant. He felt like telling Carlos to shut the fuck up or he'd throw him out of the car and leave him for dead. But instead he looked away, out through the window, and counted everything he could till he ran out of patience with counting. Sweat ran down his back, into his crack. Ants in his pants. He wriggled side to side to dry the sweat onto his jeans. He pushed hard into the seat to dry the sweat on his back. He didn't really feel hot but the speed had him sweating like a pig.

'Carlos, do pigs sweat?'

Carlos wasn't listening. Blackie dropped the subject and went about looking at the passing scenery. Everything looked the same sameness. Suburb after suburb, with its sameness of concrete and steel. The cars and shit things, turning everything into a milkshake of flash colours. And then all the towns, the yellow and green roofs. It all looked the same sameness to Blackie.

The houses blended in with their unnatural surroundings. Factories and shops and car yards and office blocks stood on cemented ground. Evergreen trees stood in place of the original gums dressing the street in an attempt to shade the smoky and filthy buildings. The trees and buildings snaked the street in crooked lines, hiding the crooked deals done to build them in the first place. It all just drifted away, as they sped past on the freeways which aren't free at all. All those roads got them tolls that the weary driver has to pay. But in the stolen car, Blackie, Rips and Carlos didn't give a fuck. They drove on past the electronic signal cameras. On they drove, on towards Wiradjuri country.

Blackie, AKA the Blackman, had a short temper at the best of times. These were not his best times – just out of gaol and broke, he decided he had to get away from city and touch the red dirt of his home country. And he had a bit of business to settle with a bastard that had kept him awake through many long nights in the Big House. Verballed by a crooked cop and gaoled for six years, Blackie had been living just to get even with the dog. Wasting little time to celebrate his release from the clink, he set out to exact payback on the verballer, Sergeant McWilliams. 'Track 'im down. Kill 'im. Track 'im down. Kill 'im …' Blackie whispered to himself in his cell. And when the time came, Blackie organised a stolen car and a dumb-arse fool by the name of Carlos (who wasn't in on the plan to kill a copper, but to do the driving) and, with his old cellmate gaolbird Rips, he hit the road.

If Carlos did the driving, Blackie figured there'd be less chance of them being stopped by highway patrol, for Carlos, although of Spanish extraction, looked like a whitefulla – straight nose, fair skin, wearing brandname clothes, and all the hallmarks Blackie reckoned of white people. Blackie and Rips were dark … Dark-skinned dark characters. There's no mistaking them two that they were not Kooris. And a Koori driving a Commodore in these country towns looks like a sure pinch by cops who assume that the Holden Commodore is the car of choice for Koori car thieves. Blackie smiled to himself now that his plans were in action.

'Carlos. How come you know that Kylie and Dannii? Ya fucken liar!'

Carlos just winked at Blackie and smiled and said, 'I know 'em, Black. I know 'em.'

They slowly cruised up the main street of Katoomba.

Katoomba is a busy place in the morning. Busy people full of business opened themselves up to another day of trade. Katoomba, the Blue Mountains boom town in New South Wales. The place where yuppies bought land and built houses to escape the heat of dirty old Sydney. But the privilege that was once the exclusive of those rich people who made it their home, eventually had come to accommodate riffraff junkies and poor people when the drug and alcohol rehabilitation centres opened in the '70s and '80s. Those same rich people spied each other with neighbourhood watch vigilance, keeping to themselves mostly in a very unneighbourly fashion.

The greengrocer, all done up like he was going to Oktoberfest – a leather apron and cap and brown shorts, carried a big orange bag filled with carrots to a wooden wheelbarrow at the front of his shop. He dumped them in, and then carried on carrying other stuff around.

A café was ready for the breakfast crowd with the doors wide open and the curtains tied back, letting in sunlight, making everything look shiny. People hungry for a pick-me-up, hanging out for their morning fix, lined up to buy. The café window had a poster with smiley people in oversized clothes and strange-looking animals on it, inviting the world to 'Step Up And See!'

Blackie acknowledged the poster with a nod.

'Circus's in town!'

Carlos looked quickly to see the sign, but missed it, and almost ran up the arse of the car in front.

'Where?'

'Look out! Fuck ya!' Blackie yelled.

Carlos was good enough to make the adjustment and missed an accident, but he missed seeing the coloured poster too, and felt left out of the action. He got his mind back on the job of driving.

But on the surface of things everything looked bright

in Katoomba to Blackie. But it wasn't his town, so he didn't care less how people treated each other there. He just wanted to get through the place as quick as possible.

Bright colours on shop walls, bright buildings, shiny glass windows reflecting brightness back onto the street. Sunshine everywhere. Sunshine bounced off leaves turning them to silhouettes, hiding their green identity from view.

Outside a chemist shop, a couple of desperate-looking characters looking poor, weak and craving stood waiting for the shop to open. They were waiting to get their morning fix too – methadone their go. The long few hours after midnight had them twitchy, anxious. Battle scars on their arms, hidden under long-sleeved shirts, cut deep into them, the result of uncounted journeys with 'Irene', holding stories of strange new places of light and dark, the slobbering, where the greatest high is found. But now, the battle-scarred slobs held their pain in their scratchy arms, crossed and tucked away from the world of bright-eyed people walking past without saying hello. They were leant against the windows, puffing madly on cigarettes, hating the light, wishing for the doors to hurry and fly open, so they could get their 'done. To be done with their aching, get off the street and slide back to whatever they had dragged themselves away from. Blackie saw them there, leaning. He gave them a nod, the car moved past. One broken-down guy looked up from looking down, and gave Blackie a half-smile.

Blackie and Carlos drove on, looking everywhere for

what was out and about. The leaning people went back to smoking, waiting, scratching.

Next door to the chemist, a big-arse church stood, demanding attention. It had a sign telling all who passed, 'Jesus Saves'.

'Ya reckon that white Jesus saves crims and car thieves? You reckon coppers and crims make up in heaven, Carlos?'

'Fucked if I know, Black. Me mum's into all that shit – church on Sundays, crosses on the walls at home. S'pose He does … They reckon He does. What do you think?'

For a while Blackie said nothing, then he answered, 'Only difference tween me and that Jesus, Carlos, is that, I'm a fuck-up!'

'Whatcha …?' Carlos asked.

He stopped the question midstream when he realised Blackie was looking elsewhere. The Spaniard followed Blackie's eyes, saw what had caught his attention. Coppers were on the road doing their morning patrol. Blackie was getting paranoid from lack of sleep and too many amphetamines. But the sight of any police car freaked him out. Better to stay out of their way, he figured … And of course, there was the little matter of the stolen car they were in to consider.

Police crept around slowly in their car, checking for odd things and 'strange fruits': for people ragged, drugged up, ripped off, acting reckless. They were on the lookout for people who moved too fast. And for people who moved too slow. And they kept an eye out for people who weren't moving at all. Their experienced scanner-eyes roamed over the street for out-of-place people up to no good. Those whose luck had run out.

'Look out for those creeps,' Blackie said without looking at the cops as they passed.

Carlos twisted his head to see, and then nodded.

'Don't look, fuck ya! Blend in.'

The cops, dressed in sharp blue shirts, wearing even sharper haircuts, drove past in the opposite direction, slowly, owned the street. They checked Blackie's car out as they did. Carlos gave them a nervous smile of hello. Blackie pretended to sneeze into his cupped hands to hide his face. He pressed his face against the dash, hiding himself away. The cops gave more than a concerting glance, assessing in a summary moment if Blackie and Carlos were worthy of an early morning questioning. But more concerned about getting to Macca's for a free coffee, the cops moved on by. The cops drove on unconcerned, though they missed their target group by inches, though they might as well have missed Blackie by a mile. They missed, that's all that mattered to the black man.

Carlos watched as best he could in his rear-view mirror until the cops had disappeared in the traffic.

'Gone?'

'Yeah ... think so. Can't see 'em,' Carlos kind of whispered, stretching his neck to see and wiping sweat from his face.

'Fucken clowns! Good. Now watch yourself 'ere, man. There's pigs everywhere in dis place. There's fucken re-abs up here – junkies everywhere. Jest dribe, slow man, like we're on our way ta work, or somethin.'

'What'll I do if they come after us, Black?' Carlos spluttered, suddenly frightened like a child.

'Take it easy, bud. Don't fucken freak out, man! Fuck ya! Be cool. We'll be right.'

Carlos nodded, but gripped the wheel a little harder, pushing his arse deeper into the seat just in case a chase was in the offing. But the cops didn't turn back. They were soon out of sight. Both groups drove on away from each other, paying attention to other things.

Young women who dressed like old men, stressed out, in pinstripes, looking sharp, walking fast, didn't look to see the nervous men in the stolen car slide right on by them. The walkers rushed to and from the railway station. Carlos slowed right down to perve a bit harder. He began humming the Eurythmics, 'Love Is a Stranger', and thought himself smart when he tricked Blackie with a loaded question, 'What is love?'

'Caring for someone, ain't it?' Blackie answered.

'Naa. It's a stranger in an open car ...' Carlos said without time to blink.

Blackie looked at him with a cockeye look and asked, 'What the fuck ya talkin bout, man?'

''Rythmics, ya know ... "Love's a stranger? ... pick you up, drive ya" ...?' Carlos sang.

Blackie laughed. 'I'll pick *you* up and chuck ya outa the fucken car in a minute if ya keep askin me stupid questions.'

There was no malice in Blackie's voice and both men had a laugh together.

Blackie watched the shiny people and thought of ants rushing hither and thither, coming and going from the nest. Blackie's eyes, sharper than the cops', saw the ordinary things in the ordinary people. Shiny people doing their ordinary things. Going to work. He saw the handbags and newspapers swinging under their arms. He noticed high heels or flats. Hidden among the ordinary, extraordinary things are playing out little games of hide and seek too. Someone once had told him about the story of the Green Ant Dreaming but though he tried, he couldn't remember any of the stories, or who told it to him. 'Fucken mind's goin to me,' he told himself.

'Fuck it,' he said. 'Sheep!' he said, looking at the walkers.

But Carlos ignored him, he had busied himself looking at women and dodging traffic. He brought the car to a full stop at the red light.

'Look there, man!' Blackie pointed.

A boy dressed in school uniform – red tie, grey socks, grey trousers, white shirt, blazer embossed with the school crest, neat short back and sides, looked to be about sixteen and the world at his feet – dropped eggs in a carton on the road in front of them. And, try as he did, the boy could not put the eggs back together again. He looked up, panicked to see the traffic lights start to flash, and ran the rest of the way across leaving the squashed mess on the road.

Blackie swung the sun visor shade down to stop the sun from getting in his eyes. It had a mirror attached to it, so he checked himself out, comparing himself to the neatly dressed kid who had just flashed across the road. There was bad history written all over his own face, and the future all over the boy's. Blackie's thick hair, that was once neatly trimmed and black as coal, was now scraggy. It had turned grey some time back.

He clenched his jaw and raised his lips to bare aching teeth that were worn from age and years of grinding. He checked his face, looking at memories written into wrinkles. Wrinkles and lines, highlighted by dirt, told tales of deeds, of a life lived. He examined closely his eyebrows and top lip – more scars there. His knuckles, battered, wore scars too. They'd turn a grey-blue when the weather was cold. Arthritis was setting in early, too bloody early for his liking. He told himself it didn't matter. Somehow it did. He tried to con himself he was too old to look pretty. He was no schoolboy with schoolboy hope, but just an old blackfulla without anything much going for him.

'Still a blackfulla,' he assured himself, and then said louder, 'I'm still black, hey Carlos?'

Carlos blinked and gulped and said, 'Yeah, man! You're Blackie!' Carlos gave him a quick sideways glance to see what he was on about but Carlos couldn't figure Blackie out. Carlos shrugged his shoulders and went back to looking at traffic and women.

★

Carlos didn't know much about Blackie's life, other than that he thought that Blackie was a smart-arse blackfulla who'd done a lot of time and had a bad temper and that he could fight. Carlos made himself useful around Blackie and the other blackfullas by way of running errands, scoring drugs for them which he always taxed, and in return, the blackfullas offered him a convenient friendship – using him whenever they could. But if any of the blacks had cottoned on to the fact that Carlos was ripping them off, even for a twenty-a-pot, they'd have knocked the cringing little bastard out cold and left him bleeding in the gutter.

'You don't even fucken know my name, man. Youse don't even know me name, bud,' Blackie said softer.

Carlos had dropped the subject. He had no idea what the fuck Blackie was on about, and he didn't give a shit about it, either.

Drugged up for the trip, Blackie began feeling that he'd like another taste. He told Carlos to drive steady, as he was gonna have a line, but then decided to wait till they were down the road a bit. Drugs had him feeling short-tempered. He began thinking about the schoolkid with the eggs again, and then thought about his own schooling. With an excellent memory, Blackie had gained first place in all of his primary school years. In the days when religious education was still being taught in public schools, Blackie came to the attention of the priests who came weekly to his school to teach the students about God. Often on the 'lookout' for a 'worthy cause', the priests contacted their bishop in Bathurst, and a bursary scholarship was offered to Blackie to attend the private school, All Hallows College in Bathurst, at the completion of his primary years. Things went well for Blackie for a while at the private school. He excelled at sport, learnt the school song, and took a keen interest in lapidary and photography and writing. But the privilege that came with the private school was a very lonely experience for him too. He was the only Koori at the school, and apart from the native Nui Guinea students, also on church scholarships, Blackie was the odd man out. The Nui Guinea boys excelled in sport and academia. But they were far from home and so banded together for company. Their friendly nature was infectious and all were highly valued across the entire school. White boys tried to get to 'take them home', to show their parents and locals these exotic black people from the north. Blackie noticed that he was never invited. He thought at first that perhaps he wasn't black enough to be thought of as something exclusive. But he learnt in time that the Nui Guinea boys were being paraded around as some kind of circus act. 'No one wants Blackie,' he told himself. 'They don't want a black bastard like me. Well, fuck 'em.'

Whether the Nui Guinea boys knew that they were 'on show' or not, Blackie didn't know. The racism was there. Blackie came to find racism on the sporting fields – '... take that, Boong!', and another knee in the back almost broke Blackie in two. 'You cunt!' Blackie muttered, in the final against another college. Yes, Blackie was called a black bastard, a nigger, a coon, a monkey, on the field, and by some people on the sidelines. And the racism was there in the classroom too. When honour days were awarded for academic achievement and behaviour each month, Blackie never got one. At seventeen years of age, Blackie stopped trying to win the prizes of the honour days, and instead, concentrated on sports. His athletic abilities were outstanding, beating the then current and former state and national champions over the 100 metres, 200 metres, in the triple jump, and the long jump and in the cross-country. 'Youse will never beat me on the field,' he declared to himself, and for his six years at boarding school, he was never beaten at his school in any race from the sprints to the long distance races. When he finally completed sixth form, he'd had enough of the competition, isolation and education, and returned to his nan's place in Dubbo and drifted towards laziness and delinquencies. A first-rate education virtually down the drain.

'And youse don't even fucken know me name!' he said to the passing world.

Driving in silence, Blackie and Carlos were lost in their own thoughts, and lost to the continuous white line. As he rolled around in a sex-fuelled dream on the back seat no one heard Rips whisper in his sleep, 'Fuck you, baby. Ahh ... fuck me. Yeah!'

Carlos and Blackie both gasped at seeing a white swan, with its beak over the neck of a black one, in a violent struggle in front of the colourful garden gnomes. The black swan fought back, flapping its wings, lashing out with its feet, trying to fly away, screaming to the gnomes for help. But the white swan had it in its grip, hard. And it looked as though it was not going to let go regardless of gnomes or anything else. Blackie wound his window down as fast as he could, and yelled, 'Fuck off, ya white cunt!'

People on the street huddled closer together and looked away from Blackie, the angry man, pretending that they could not see anything. They quickly moved further away from the violence, keeping safe. Trying to make themselves invisible.

Blackie didn't look back to see the black swan escape, a little worse for wear and tear from the fight, but still alive and kicking.

'Fuck Katoomba. Shithouse town that dump, hey mate?' Blackie said to Carlos when they hit the highway, leaving the hurrying people and fighting swans behind them.

'Sure is, bud. Took Mimi up there once, though. Seen the Three Sisters. Stayed at the Hydro, brother,' Carlos bragged.

'Who?' Blackie asked, unconvinced.

'Mimi ... Mimi Macpherson, you know? Elle's sister,' Carlos replied.

Blackie didn't believe him. He wondered how this guy would ever be able to hang with those rich people, Blackie had no idea. Blackie didn't know rich people ... Blackie wasn't rich. And Carlos wasn't rich. But Blackie knew that the Spaniard had rich dreams and big ideas and stuff. Blackie decided that perhaps Carlos 'dreamt' the Minogue sisters, and the Antz Pantz woman and the Macpherson women. They, in reality, were little more than dreams to poor boys like them anyway.

'Did ya fuck dem Three Sisters, too?' Blackie asked. 'Did ya fuck the Blue Mountains, man?'

'Blaaaack! Can't fuck a mountain!' Carlos laughed.

'You sure bout that, man? You whitefullas sure fucked my country. Youse fucked her alright,' Blackie said.

2

Remembering and Forgetting

Blackie and Carlos fell into their own private thoughts for a while, as the radio songs kept the rhythm of the relationship. Blackie nodded his head and looked away and went back to trying to count road signs as they passed, but the signs passed too fast to count, so he gave up. Carlos, lost in his own thoughts, nodded his head in time with the radio playing The Doors classic 'L.A. Woman'.

Blackie dedicated some time to trying to remember what Green Ant Dreaming was all about. But he couldn't remember *who* told him about the legend, and he couldn't, for the life of him, remember *where* he heard the story. But he couldn't get it back in his head either, so he decided to give up thinking about it for the time being. Maybe later, he thought, the Dreaming would come back to him. So he closed his eyes to rest. While resting, he thought again of Fanon's words, and of Fanon's great gift of knowledge to the world. The shrink gave Blackie a copy of Fanon's bestseller *Black Skin, White Masks* to read when Blackie was doing time at Silverwater gaol. Blackie loved the book and told his friends about the black man, Fanon – the doctor, the revolutionary. Blackie quoted a favourite passage to himself – a white man is speaking:

'Oh, I know the blacks. They must be spoken to kindly; talk to them about their country; it's all in knowing how to talk to them.'

Carlos heard Blackie mumbling. Carlos looked across to see Blackie, eyes shut, talking to himself. Carlos didn't know how to speak to someone who was there, but wasn't, so he looked away and said nothing.

But Blackie was busy in thought. He thought of Fanon's greatness and extraordinariness. Blackie thought himself to be just an ordinary black. Blackie had no great gifts to give the world. Anyway, if he did have such gifts, they were hidden away, so far away, deep down inside himself, that he couldn't find them.

'I'm broken, Carlos,' he said softly, way too softly for Carlos to hear over Jimmy Barnes singing 'Flame Trees' on the radio.

Blackie was broke. Broken and running into the gutter, and the songs in his head accompanied him throughout his life journeys, giving a rhythm to his footsteps.

He tried to sleep, but Jimmy was turned up too loud. So he sat up and tried to count things again.

The bush looked so beautiful. Even the planted pine trees appeared serene.

Blackie watched the pines, all khaki green, standing there, in their soldier lines, waiting for the wood chopper to cut them all down.

The trees looked from behind their leaves at the boys flying past but the trees kept quiet about it.

Lithgow was just up the road a bit from where they were, and getting closer all the while.

L 40

L 35

L 30

L 25

As Rips continued snoring on the back seat, Blackie looked out the window hoping to see a kangaroo. But there were none to be seen. Crushed and still by the roadside, a spiny echidna lay dead. All stiff, like beaten egg whites, the poor thing was there, but it wasn't there. Its soul had left its body the moment the hand of death touched it. Now, there it lay. Decaying. Returning to the eternal Mother. Back on the path, the echidna doesn't need eyes to see the way. That pathway is the free trip all the dead discover, leaving only a carcass behind, to return to its place of origin … to the Mother … Back to earth. Blackie knew this.

The smell of the dead animal flooded in on the wind and smothered the air inside the car. Blackie coughed the stench of death out from his lungs, only to breathe it back in again. The smell made him cough and cough and cough. He reached for the drugs in the esky.

'Slow down, bra.'

Carlos moved into the outside lane and dropped the car back to a crawl while Blackie did his thing. Blackie had a good, big lot, swallowing it in one gulp, and cursing about the state of his affairs to himself as he did. With hungry eyes, Carlos looked to see if he could have some.

Blackie saw him, 'Wait'll we git up here a bit, bud, give ya some then, ay? Don't want highway patrol crashin our party, hey?'

Carlos begrudgingly agreed that would be a bad thing, so he put his foot down on the pedal.

Just then, crackling over the air waves, they heard the cruisy voice of Ray Charles, singing 'Hit the Road Jack'.

They sang in unison. Ray Charles' spirit cruised with them for a while, singing the song of goodbye with them as they drove away from the dead echidna.

Driving through the Blue Mountains (slippery with its crying rock faces and deep valleys, and filled with mysteries) is an experience to behold. Everything slips away in a blur of colours. The symmetry of water, rock, wood and earth, caressed by wind, whips around and through everything. That land, known first by blackfullas, holds knowledge in every moment – beneath every shadow.

But that same land slipped away too fast for the men in the car to appreciate for more than a few fleeting seconds.

On the men drove, with Blackie on speed, and Carlos speeding too fast for the poor old Mother Earth to keep up. As the green and grey bush flew by, Blackie went back to summing up his life to himself. He painted himself a black picture … grim and lonely. Friends dumped him because of his constant fight against the system. But to Blackie it was the system that was always at war with him. 'Why ya gotta always be lookin for fight with the whitefullas, Black? Ya jest lookin for trouble all the time when ya do, boy,' his family warned him. They just wanted to get on with getting on with the world.

But not Blackie. 'Fuck it, man! Them whitefullas should pay for what they've done,' was Blackie's response.

When he was in gaol, he'd begun to prepare himself for what he thought would be the fight of his life. He wanted a showdown with the policeman, McWilliams.

Blackie got his head together. He thought about and concentrated on remembering McWilliams. He imagined how he'd make McWilliams beg for mercy. Blackie sweated in his cell, doing 1000 push-ups a day. In the yard he ran the fence line, getting lung capacity and strong legs from the exercise. At night he rested, knowing that he'd be as fit as a fiddle by the time he got released.

'Fuck you, McWilliams,' he whispered as the car drove the twisty bends.

Blackie was gonna git himself some payback on the dog that sent him away – he was gonna pay back that pig that verballed him! And Blackie had it set in his head that that pig would squeal.

'Gonna hurt you, McWilliams, BAD – real fucken BAD!'

After that, well, Blackie would just have to take it like a man, no matter where the chips fell. If they got him, if he got gaoled again, then that would be that. At least he would have paid back that copper dog. He tried to convince himself that he didn't care. He had grown tougher on the inside. Completed what he called a postgraduate degree, yet another graduate from that old school of hard knocks. He pumped weights and sparred with others in gaol. He mixed it with men who could use their dukes. He mixed it with them all. From flyweights through to overweights, he boxed and sweated and kept his mind on McWilliams, imagining how he would hurt the cop with every punch he threw.

At Cessnock he was accused of thieving from another's cell. Blackie got wild and dropped the bloke who accused him of the crime he didn't commit. He broke the other man's jaw. The blackfullas all cheered and had their blood up too, ready to take on any who stepped forward to attack Blackie. The screws intervened and charged Blackie with GBH. But when it got to court in Maitland, there were no witnesses to the event. But after court, the screws moved him from Cessnock to the maximum security gaol of Maitland, and then, eventually back to Silverwater.

When it all came down to it, Blackie had a bad attitude. He'd use whatever it took to win. A chair over the head, an iron bar across the face, a pool cue, and the old sandshoe shuffle – whatever it took, Blackie would use if available. He knew that it wasn't the way for a *man* to fight. Blackie knew that it was fear that produced that kind of reaction.

'Fuck it!' he swore out through the open window.

In Dubbo, he reckoned, he'd face life with death, and see who blinked first.

He lit a smoke and threw the packet in Carlos' lap. Carlos lit up, and threw the packet back. The radio had music playing, but neither man was listening. The world rushing by was a world away to them. Blackie's thoughts found him wondering about where he'd meet McWilliams.

But Carlos wasn't paying attention for Carlos' mind was on happier times.

'Hey, Carlos,' Blackie piped up. 'I was born on the same day as a bloke who's a copper up here in Dubbo, ya know?'

'Yeah, man?' Carlos replied.

'Yep. I grew up with him. We useda shake apples together – the thievin bastard. Now he's a fucken crooked cop!' Blackie said.

'Was he your mate?'

'Thought he was. Not now.'

Blackie turned to look at Rips on the back seat. Seeing him sound asleep in an uncomfortable position, all scrunched up, mouth open, eyes half shut, Blackie asked, 'How can a bloke sleep like *that*?'

'Drunk!'

Blackie shook his head, then turned back to watch the rushing road flying up towards them.

'Pull over, man. Gotta piss,' he said. The urge to piss had come on suddenly. He got out and scarpered to the bush, and relieved himself.

Cruising the highway was a pious policeman – Gatherbee. His morning was the same as yesterday, nothing happening. Passing Carlos sitting at the driver's seat parked on the side of the road, Gatherbee did a quick U-turn to check out if there were any problems.

Blackie hearing the squeal of tyres on the road glanced back, frightened by the sound of the policeman's tyres on the cold road.

'Fuck!' Blackie whispered when he saw the highway patrol car stop beside Carlos.

Blackie thought, 'What if the copper gets out of the car, and sees Rips asleep not wearing a seat belt?' Just a little thing like that would give the cop a reason to wake the sleeping man:

To issue a ticket …

That requires a name.

That demands a police check.

That would show that Rips has a first instance warrant out on him.

That means an arrest …

That means more cops …

That means they'd pinch him and Carlos too for the stolen car.

And that'd mean that he'd never get to see McWilliams, or his grandmother's country, again.

'Fuck-me-dead!' Blackie cursed.

But the policeman didn't bother to get out of his car. Through the open window of his patrol car, Gatherbee asked Carlos if he needed a hand. Relieved, Carlos answered that he was alright, that he was just waiting for his mate to finish his business, nodding his head towards Blackie. Carlos didn't take his eyes off the policeman for a second. He was looking for any indication that the cop was onto them. Any subtle movement by the cop would have Carlos ram the police car and try an escape, leaving Blackie there with his dick out, to fight his own battle. Alone. Carlos could hardly breathe. His hands sweated and he kept re-gripping the steering wheel to get a better hold, thinking that his number was up and the copper would be in an arresting mood.

'Don't wake up, Rips! Don't bloody wake up, man,' Carlos prayed.

Gatherbee saw Blackie there, pissing. The policeman, satisfied that everything was on the up and up, nodded, turned his cruiser around, squealing the tyres, and sped off again down the road in the opposite direction.

'Phew! Faaarrrk!' Carlos breathed. He released his grip on the wheel, wiggled his tense fingers, then wiped his brow as Blackie got back in and slammed the door.

'Shit! Git outa here, man,' Blackie ordered.

Blackie didn't have to tell Carlos twice. The Spaniard put the pedal to the metal and spun the wheels, fish-tailing it back onto the black-tarred road.

It took ten kilometres before Blackie spoke again.

'Lucky that Rips never woke up, hey bud?'

''Ken oath,' Carlos agreed.

Blackie got back to telling him about McWilliams.

'That copper bloke I wuz tellin ya, Carlos. He's a

jealous bastard, man. Real mean streak in him. Wuz always trying ta beat me …'

Carlos nodded, and asked for a smoke. Blackie lit a cigarette, took a couple of drags and then passed it to Carlos.

'Yeah. Could never beat me in a fair go, the cheatin bastard. McWilliams would drop his shoulder at the startin line when he was next ta me ta git me ta jump-the-gun and git disqualified. Bet, he could never beat me,' Blackie laughed. 'He'd be out there trainin all the time. I'd be off with me mates down the river, somewhere … still useda beat him.'

'How'd he take that?' Carlos asked, now interested in Blackie's yarn.

'Fucken hated it. Know what we useda call him?'

'Naa. What?'

'Well, with a name like McWilliams, we called him Red Label, ya know? Red label McWilliams – flagons a port? He fucken hated it, too. I heard him sayin one day:

Jacky, Jacky
Fucken Blackie!
I'll get you one day

I still remember that! Cunt got me alright.'

Blackie twisted uncomfortably in his seat, sticky from sweat and rememberings.

'Yeah? Did he?' Carlos asked, puffing away on the cigarette. 'How'd he go against you?' he asked.

'That prick never beat me! … Didn't stop him tryin though. He's a dog! I'm gonna fucken smash him when I see him!'

‘Why, Black? What’d he do?’ Carlos asked, guessing correctly that there was more to the story than Blackie had revealed.

‘Verballed me, man. Loaded me up with bullshit drug charges. I jest done six years over that man. He’s fucken going down, brother!’

3

White Lines

Blackie was high on the speed as they flew through dirty old Lithgow, without giving it a second thought.

Back out on the freeway, Blackie was in a better mood, and decided to give Carlos a line before they hit Bathurst.

'Pull up, man. Wanna do another piss. Give ya a line, hey?'

'Thanks, brother,' the grateful Carlos spoke.

He parked the car on the side, near bushes, and waited until Blackie finished his business out there before he spoke again.

'I'll keep an eye out for the pigs, Black.'

Blackie grunted and got busy getting Carlos a bit of speed.

''Ere, cuz ... Git dis into ya,' Blackie said with a smile.

Carlos gulped it down in one go, and then drank from his bottle of water, smiling, nodding and thanking Blackie with his eyebrows raised.

'How far to Bathurst, Carlos?' Blackie asked as they drove away from the bushy place of shadows and wind, into misty rain.

'Not far, mate. Bout twenty-five,' Carlos answered.

The air got cold and the rain got heavy. Big splashy blobs of water exploded across the windscreen as they drove down from the escarpment. Bathurst was laid out like a jigsaw below them.

The bush was cut right back from their four-lane highway, to give clear space for service vehicles and the giant power cable rigs that ran away out of sight to signal boxes and other modern things. That ground is cold and stony. Grey is the colour of most days. Grey misty days. Grey ground. Grey rocks. Grey clouds. Grey, grey, greyer in some places grey and sad.

No ceremonial earth dances take place at the top of the mountain now. The old dancers left that place of dreaming when the white people came through with gun, cutlass and the Bible. New dreamers now, in cars and trucks, on trains and in biker lines, dreamers wearing fluoro gear, other men on tractors and crap, sped through the mountain there, slicing the songline to ribbons, killing the dream, and hurting the Mother Earth.

Forgotten by many, that beautiful place now cries alone all night long for her dancers to come back and step softly, to sing to the old Mother Earth. She waits there, scarred and bleeding, waiting to be admired again by her children. Waiting to once again be the centre of the world.

A pine forest, planted on one side of the road. All the trees shiver when the wind blows. The pines cry too. They sob like stolen children did when the boss came for them – them pines. They tremble when the chainsaw begins to rip through their brothers' trunks. They shiver and tremble each time they hear a truck coming, thinking that it might be coming to take them. So, they stand there perfectly uniform, perfectly still. They are scared, hoping that no one will pick them. Brave but too weak to defend themselves against a saw, they tremble beneath the bark. The pines stand alone, together.

Standing so very still in the rain, the pines watched and breathed a sigh of relief as the men drove on by without stopping.

When the men hit the outskirts of Bathurst, Blackie stiffened up and sat fully upright to see the city he'd gone to high school at once more.

Blackie said with a fixed stare, 'Hate dis fucken place!'

His eyes were shiny like opals from the speed he'd taken back before Lithgow. He was off his head a little.

'Yeah? Why's that?' Carlos asked.

Blackie thought of frontier wars he'd read about in history books. He thought about the great Wiradjuri leader Windradyne and thought again of Fanon. He wondered what those two would say to each other.

Lost in thought, Blackie didn't hear the question, and continued to speak over the top of Carlos.

'Whitefullas slaughtered blacks here, after Wentworth, Blaxland and Lawson found a way across. Dis is all fucken blood-land 'ere, man!'

They came to the old showground. It was like he

remembered it when he went there to race white runners as a kid. The wooden fence still needed a coat of paint. Memories of excited kids and ice creams on the ground, memories of cheering and winning came back to him in a rush making him choke back tears.

'On your mark! Set!' … *Bang*! went the gun, and, the runners raced away towards a finish line. First – the blue ribbon, second – the red ribbon, third – the green ribbon. Blackie smiled. 'Used ta race here when I was at school, Carlos,' he said as they drove past the showground.

'Yeah,' Carlos replied.

Blackie dropped the memory talk and looked away out through the window.

Bathurst is green. Green grass everywhere in that town. The fields near the river, where Wiradjuri women once sat and sang to their children, where men, back from fishing, lay back to stretch their backs, where black boys tested their arms with sticks, copying the old men throwing spears, hide stories. Recent ones. Stories of conquest and resistance, bloodstains. Bloodstains everywhere there in that place, if you look hard enough. But the blood has dried and is covered by lawns and food crops. The stories are buried.

Buried from

v

i

e

w

'Git me outa 'ere, man! Me and 'im did a lota hard time in this hole,' Blackie said, nodding towards Rips, and then pointing down the road, 'Go dis way.'

They took the old road out. Not the new one that runs up past the gaol. The old road. Out past All Hallows School, on the old road near the river, out past the row of poplar trees, where the magpies delight in dive-bombing the schoolkids in the spring. The men drove out past the scary old house on the overgrown estate, past the side road that runs up the back way to the cemetery and on to the gaol. Out past the Eglinton turn-off they went, fast, and on up around the bend they flew towards Orange.

Blackie's thoughts returned to McWilliams. McWilliams with the square face and lazy eye. McWilliams the red-face, always trying to hide his rage from the world. McWilliams the jealous man.

'Yeah man. Ole "Red Label" was jealous of everything! 'Specially me,' Blackie said.

It made McWilliams as mad as hell. He swore that he wasn't gonna take it anymore! He thought that no one knew of his jealous heart. It was a heavy weight. And it hurt him like carrying a sack of stones. But it fuelled his rage and determination more than anything else. He made promises to himself that he'd get Blackie one day, no matter how long it took him. He'd get 'em all back for laughing at him, making him feel small.

And now a crown sergeant, he thought he was King Shit! They'd all take notice now, he told himself. He had dreams of climbing the ladder. He did things he wasn't supposed to do to get ahead. He took credit for the labour of others. He cheated and he lied. He worked slyly and he worked hard.

All that loneliness as a kid made him more determined and fragile than most. A man who hid himself behind his badge and his uniform. He coached kids in football in his spare time, and spoke to old people about community watch programs. The general population saw him as a great guy and yet the same guy kicked the shit out of drunks when no one was looking. Beneath his blue police uniform and awards, a crook lurked and waited for his turn to make it big.

When the opportunity came to nab Blackie, McWilliams seized his opportunity with both hands. He accused him of supplying narcotics. Blackie fell in the shit. He didn't stand a chance in court. He went down hard. Dropped without a prayer. As the Queen looked down from her glass frame upon her black subject, Blackie got nine years with a non-parole period of six. 'Got ya now, you black cunt,' McWilliams mouthed, when the sentence came down from the bench.

'Get fucked, you white cunt!' Blackie mouthed back from the dock.

McWilliams smiled an ugly victory smile as they led Blackie away and spent the afternoon drinking single malt whisky with his mates at the RSL.

Blackie spent the rest of his day sulking and pacing the watch house floor, refusing bread and water.

The truck took him next day to Silverwater, and his long sentence began in stormy weather.

Blackie served every day of the sentence with McWilliams on his mind.

Blackie didn't contest the charge, like some other people might have. He suffered silently, grew wild. He didn't forget McWilliams for a minute. And he didn't forgive, like he'd seen other blackfullas do once they got into their sentence. All those guys wanted were to be out again and do it all over again. Party animals, those guys. But the party was over for Blackie. He just waited and waited for the day he'd see McWilliams again. He got fit. And then he got fitter! He walked the clean floor of B Wing like he was king. Men stepped aside, and screws watched him carefully, raided his room and searched his hole.

Time passed slowly.

Years followed years.

But finally, Blackie was out.

'I'm still just a Blackie Blackie,' he murmured, 'but you're the real fucken pig, ya copper bastard! I'll see you soon, you fuck! Count on it, cunt!'

'Wonder if big-arse there is gonna wake up 'fore we hit Dubbo?' Blackie asked aloud.

Blackie hummed a verse from the great Roy Buchanan blues number to himself, 'Roy's Blues'. 'Roy's Blues' could have been written for him.

★

After a while, Carlos took up the conversation again.

'You grow up with Rips, Black?'

'Naa … met him in gaol, man.'

'What was he in for?'

'Killed someone … by mistake …' Blackie answered softly.

Blackie leant back and smoked as he spoke about meeting Rips in gaol for the first time and how a quick friendship grew between the two of them. Blackie remembered that it was a hot day in summer when he arrived at Silverwater. The first person he saw when his feet hit the ground from the transport truck was a stocky blackfulla with a smile a mile wide it seemed, leaning against the fence. 'Cuz, where you from?' a blackfulla called to Blackie.

'Dubbo, bra. What bout you?' Blackie answered as he went through the gate.

'Wild Gate, brother,' Rips replied, meaning he was from Walgett.

And because the two were from the western district, that was all it took for the two to form alliance. Rips showed Blackie around and kicked the other guy who was sharing his cell out on his ear, telling him to find another bed, and, just like that, Blackie moved in. The two black men shared a friendship based upon similar cultural backgrounds and stood beside each other if trouble or fights came their way.

Carlos was stoking the old Commodore up as they roared on towards Lucknow, doing over a hundred kilometres an hour. The land reminded Blackie so much of his past. It held secrets, too, he felt there were ghosts all around. Everything came back in flashes of green and grey as the bush flew by.

He used to visit Lucknow as a kid, on school excursions. It was an exciting place to get lost for a while.

Lucknow is just a little place now, just outside the city of Orange. It clings to the side of the highway, like moss to a rock. Lucknow, that small place that grew out of the Wentworth estate, rich with the yellow metal! It was once a thriving town, cashed up and full of action. Men rushed there to search for the flash of yellow in their pans. It was noisy with the work of shovels, with people grunting and swearing in despair, and in joy when they got lucky. While the rush was on, it was the place to be for the white people.

Just a few seconds' drive-through on the road to a bigger place now though.

Before the white people, Lucknow was a quiet place where Wiradjuri people rested. And before that: it was a place where Rainbow Snake rested on the great river-making journey. It became the place where old Wiradjuri men told stories of the Dreaming to their children at evening time. Large mobs of grey kangaroos hopped over rock ground, huge flocks of black cockatoos blocked out the sun.

Wiradjuri people remember Lucknow as their homeland, a place taken from them in a violent land grab. And they know it was Rainbow Snake's resting place. The white people desecrated and disgraced that place, and the Wiradjuri people saw white people value it in the economic but not in the spiritual way. So the Snake Dreaming place got dirty with waste and rubbish to stand there now completely overgrown, overlooked, and mostly forgotten.

The ghosts of old Wiradjuri linger there though, and, if you're quiet – very quiet – those ghosts will visit you sometimes. They'll come around, those ghosts will, if you go poking around beside the old streams. You might feel their ghostly presence in the icy wind that blows up under your hair, behind your collar, in the afternoons when camp fires are lit. The ghosts look at the visitors from the trees. They wait there. They wait for the return of the Wiradjuri people, those ghosts, to hear black kids playing in the water.

Blackie looked but didn't see any ghosts by the road, though he thought that ghosts still hung around. He smelt their sweet smell as they drove past.

'Git away from here, bud,' Blackie crossed his arms and held himself tight together, 'too many fucken ghosts!'

Carlos eased the car back into the single lane.

'Hope we have good luck, Carlos. Highway patrol all long 'ere, man. Watch it, bud,' Blackie warned.

Carlos slowed down and looked too; he couldn't see any cops or ghosts hiding behind signs or trees. So he gunned it up around the bend. The car engine screamed loudly as up around the sweeping bend they raced. They drove along quietly for a while, lost in thought. Then they slipped by Orange in the light rain, taking the side road out of town towards Wellington, unseen.

'Yeah, man,' Blackie continued, 'met Rips in gaol. He accidentally killed his girlfriend when he was young. Hit her by mistake one night, when he was fightin another bloke. She jumped in between 'em to stop 'em, and he dropped her by mistake. Died from hitting her head on the gutter.'

'Fuck!' gulped Carlos.

'Yeah … fuck, alright,' Blackie agreed.

Rips loved her. Yeah, everything was sweet between those two lovers. It was serious love between them two, you know?

And yet, Rips killed the girl – smashing his young love in the gutter. All that's left of it now is her memory, the bloodstain on the cement. Her ghost was Rips' secret companion. She was always there, hanging round in his head, invading his dreams and waking him up. Nothing could hold her spirit down. She'd slip straight through the bars of every cell he slept in. Through the walls of the buildings, she'd come. She'd sit there at the foot of his bed and look at him. He'd asked her for forgiveness a million times.

She'd just sit there.

He cried when no one was looking.

'Ya know, cops barred him from his hometown, Carlos?' Blackie said.

'Yeah? What for?'

'Cause they can. Said they wuz worried about fights tween the families,' Blackie answered, and opened another beer.

Carlos knew the story about Rips and the killing of his girlfriend, he heard it from others when they were bongin-on around the fire at Mascot, but he wanted to know more.

Carlos, the busybody, was always on the lookout for stories about people so that he might incorporate them into his own pretend life when talking to impress people he met. But Blackie said no more on the matter.

Blackie remembered Rips telling him how payback after payback took its turn between the families over the years.

'Everyone got it, bra,' Rips told him. 'Dey always fightin back 'ome over me, bud.'

But no one suffered more than the girl's mother.

Once in a blue moon, Rips'd sneak back to the little dusty town of his birth, under the cover of darkness, to see his own old mother, and some of his closest relatives.

Carlos lit a smoke, and the smoke went down the wrong way, making him choke on it, making Blackie laugh. Blackie suddenly thought of the US president Clinton, and smiled.

'Fucken liar, hey Carlos?' Blackie asked.

'Who, bra?' Carlos asked, watery-eyed and sniffling.

'Clinton! The fucker ... Remember ... "Yes I smoked mar-it-chew-warrn-na. But I did not inhale!" Remember him saying that?'

'Naa. Not really, bud. Dunno anyone named Clinton,' Carlos said.

'You idiot!' Blackie scoffed. 'He was an American president.'

'Ahh, him ... yeah. I remember him ...' Carlos bullshitted.

Clinton might not have inhaled, but Rips did – big time! Blackie told the story about the bouncers who were trying to stand over a little old chap who had done all his dough on the horses and the pokies. The Cauliflower Hotel on Botany Road was always full of music and people on Saturday nights. It was the place to be to pick up women, men and drugs. Bouncers stood at the door and stood over those they could in order to impress mostly newcomers to the pub – those who'd heard what a swingin joint it was. The bouncers were making a joke outa the old fella. They were show-offs, full of muscles and steroids. Full of themselves. Full of shit, man. The old man happened to be in that dingy bar that time and that was the wrong bar at the wrong time. The bouncers thought that they'd get a cheap victory.

That was until the Big Rips made it his business to be the old chap's champion. Rips hated bouncers. He couldn't stand stand-overs. He hated all them in their uniforms, with their arms full of tatts.

And so, trying to sound like Mr T in that *Rocky* movie, Rips challenged the bouncers to 'come over 'ere an abba crack at a real man, not a old pensioner!'

★

The bouncers didn't like that much. And so it was on. But Rips dropped them. Both of them. The bouncers were out cold and bleeding. Big, bad Rips then pulled out his big, black dick and pissed all over their heads, right there on the street in front of everyone. By the time Blackie got to the brawl it was all over, and Rips was standing there, bare-chested, smiling broadly, and pissing freely, showing all and sundry his cock.

'Fuck! Sooo funny, man ...' Blackie laughed, remembering the gasps of disgust from the women who'd seen the whole affair.

'He escaped from custody once, Rips did,' Blackie continued. 'Held cops at bay for a long time. Hmm. True, man! They bought the Rapid Response Group in to deal with that one, brother.'

A cop finally talked sense into Rips, and he gave himself up in the early morning light. Coppers kicked his guts in behind the cars, outa sight. Another two-year sentence went onto his original term. They sent him to hell.

Off to Lithgow he went.

Off to solitary.

By the time he got out, he was fucked.

4

Becoming Wiradjuri

Blackie looked out on the overcast afternoon sky. He stared at the Blue Mountains that were drippy-wet from dew and rain. Those mountains are hard – hard like Rips, Blackie thought to himself. Hard and cold and wet – crying. They are grey with age and green with moss, and even though they are dirty from cars and exhaust fumes, and dirty from graffiti, from life, the mountains in Wiradjuri country are still the most beautiful. And the mountains are still sacred.

'Listen, Black … I gotta do a piss, man,' Carlos said, seeming like he was sick of listening to Blackie's reminiscing. 'Let's get off this main road, man. Isn't there a back road we can take? If we get caught, man! Faaark! Don't need *that*, brother.'

'No, stay on this road! Cops spot us out there on them back roads … Stand out like dogs' balls, man. Stay 'ere – blend in, man! Stop up here at Geurie, brother,' Blackie said, pointing ahead and getting itchy feet now that Dubbo was in range.

Carlos looked at Blackie, nodded, but said nothing.

Suddenly exasperated, Blackie said to thin air, 'Outa fucken sight, man!'

Thoughts flying round like mad galahs had Blackie's mind here, there and everywhere. His thoughts flew to the graveside of his friend, the cripple, Crusoe. Poor little Crusoe, disabled from birth with spina bifida, he walked with crutches and was always in pain. It was a deliberate overdose from a highball that finally did him in, at the grand old age of twenty-one.

Crusoe, or Cruzzie as Blackie called him, used to sell pot from his mother's house on the Mission at La Perouse. Blackie gave him protection when he told Blackie that young fullas were robbing him and breaking into the house.

'Who are the dogs, cuz?' Blackie asked.

Crusoe told him that they were local boys who lived nearby who had always liked picking on him. Crusoe had suffered their bullying for years. Blackie grew wild and went looking for the thieving bullies. He found the group of youths, drinking behind the boatshed. Blackie wasted no time at all and dropped the biggest thief with two punches. The rest stood back, afraid. The boy who lay bleeding in the dust had tears in his eyes from pain and shame. The boy's father came rushing in when he heard from a girl who had witnessed the fiasco that Blackie had hit his boy. Blackie turned and shaped up to the father and dropped him in two hits also. 'Fucken come near Crusoe's again, I'll kill youse. I'll kill the fucken lota youse. Ya fucken dogs – stealin from cripples!

Ya weak cunts!' Blackie screamed, standing shirtless with blood on his hands, looking scary as a monster. Crusoe stood beside Blackie and in the excitement of the fighting threw his crutches to the ground and tore his shirt from his twisted body too, struggling to stand, to shape up. And, though Cruzzie would have been a pushover, his bravery was a magnificent sight that was long spoken of after that day.

'Tan, tan, tanks, Black,' he said, tearing up.

'You sweet, bra. Anytime, man,' was all Blackie said and a forever friendship was forged between the two men, right there on the spot.

To Blackie, Cruzzie was the little brother he'd never had. To Crusoe, Blackie was the big brother he'd always wished he had. The two were inseparable for the remaining two years Crusoe lived and his death crushed Blackie. Cruzzie visited Blackie at Long Bay gaol when he was on remand, bringing him cash for gaol buy-ups, keeping him informed of community activities. When Crusoe died the officers brought Blackie to the graveside in cuffs. He wore a new white shirt, shiny shoes and black trousers, looking so sad and magnificently Aboriginal at the same time. At the graveside Blackie said, 'He's at peace now, Aunt. No more shit from this place for him … He was my brother …'

The death of young Aboriginal people from suicides, from overdoses, from deaths in custody really troubled Blackie. Young men in gaol necked themselves and he was witness to the bodies, covered in sheets, being carried out of the cells a few times. The sight of the dead men scared Blackie and saddened him as he thought of the darkness they may have felt that pushed them to suicide. He wondered if he'd go the same way.

'Too many young fullas. Too many young fullas!' Blackie yelled, and suddenly punched the dashboard. He hit the dash so hard it buckled a little. He hit it hard, just like he'd hit McWilliams once he saw him. The punch made Carlos lose control of the car.

'Hey! Watch how ya drivin there man, fuck ya!' Blackie yelled, feeling the car swaying towards the edge.

'Fuck, Black!' Carlos said. 'Nearly pissed meself.'

Blackie smirked, but didn't say anything. Geurie was just around the bend.

Carlos sweated and nodded, correcting his mistake, quietly smiling.

Carlos checked his rear-vision mirror for traffic, and checked himself out at the same time.

The miles raced past. Blackie liked being chauffeured. As he watched the landscape change from the hard rocky granite land of the mountains, to the soft green rolling hills of the central west, his mind wandered.

He thought of all the speed he had swallowed. He knew that pretty soon he'd want some more. And then more. And more. And, more and more, and ... Faces of old friends and images of places he'd not seen in years came flooding back in a scrambled mess. He hardly knew what was real anymore.

★

They hit Geurie in a hurry, but stopped for Carlos, for his cigarettes and to do a piss.

Geurie is a sleepy hamlet, less than 500 people live there. It's a tiny place, hanging on between Orange and Wellington. Trains stop to collect wool bales and crops and farmers' kids, taking them away to other places. The emptiness of Geurie belies great wealth. There's rich farming land all around, with plenty of sweet water and fertile soil: ideal sheep and cropping country.

They stopped and Blackie got out and stretched his legs, then followed Carlos into the shop. Carlos stopped inside the doorway and pretended to check out the magazine rack, decided that a few lollies and a yo-yo were within reach for an easy pinch. As Blackie made his way to the counter and bought cigarettes, Carlos made his move. But, even though the old woman wore glasses, she spotted what Carlos was up to. She deftly pressed a button beneath the counter. It rang a bell out the back where her son sat doing the company books. Her son appeared just as Carlos revved the car. The son chased, but couldn't catch up. Carlos laughed and sped away, chewing on one of his chocolate éclair lollies.

'Ya bloody idiot! Whatcha do that for?'

Blackie ran his closed fist and threatened to punch Carlos' face in.

Carlos looked confused.

'What? It's only shit … Look,' Carlos said.

Blackie didn't care what Carlos had stolen.

'Don't tell me you haven't pinched anything, Black? There's no cops in that dump!' Carlos assured.

Blackie closed his fist and felt like smashing Carlos. But he held his temper and looked away.

'Sorry, brother,' Carlos said, now regretting that which he'd done.

'Sorry be fucked!' Blackie yelled.

Carlos offered lollies to Blackie, Blackie snatched them and threw them out the window. Blackie grabbed the yo-yo before Carlos could blink and chucked it too.

Blackie hoped that the man who chased them might find the lollies and yo-yo, and things would be square again. But it was pretty unlikely. Carlos was too afraid to say anything, so he kept his eyes on the road and drove a little faster than before, just to get as far away from Geurie as he could.

Blackie knew that there was not any use of carrying on about what Carlos had done now. The deed had been done, and that was that. He shrugged his shoulders and decided that he'd just have to accept whatever the future would bring.

'Fuckwit!' he said to himself, thinking of Carlos.

Time slipped by and Blackie calmed down.

Looking through the window Blackie smiled and said proudly, 'This was my grandmother's country round 'ere.'

He looked at the rose-red rocks – his grandmother's magnificent homeland – the red land was older than time itself. As he spoke, he moved his hand in a gesture across the windscreen, as if to show it was his country too.

Carlos saw it as an opening.

'What tribe was she from?' he asked.

Carlos knew enough about Kooris that family was everything to them. And he knew that their grannies were at the top of those black men's respect.

Blackie heard Rips stirring in the back.

Blackie kept his eyes looking ahead for police cars, he softly answered,

'Wiradjuri. She was Rad-jree, man. She lived till she was nearly a 'undred years old. It's not tribe, Carlos, it's language group.'

He didn't want to talk anymore. He just wanted to think about his dead grandmother, and of old songs she loved. He hummed the country song 'Pick Me Up on Your Way Down'.

Carlos must have read Blackie's body language, and didn't follow up with further questions. Blackie remembered his grandmother's smile and the old glasses she wore. He thought of the old woman back in the shop that Carlos had stolen from.

'Fuck ya, Carlos ... Why'd ya steal from that old woman?' he asked.

But Carlos just blinked and said nothing. Blackie felt like smashing Carlos again, but held himself back. He hated himself for taking Carlos through Geurie. He hated himself for being an addict. He hated himself for being Blackie.

If he had been normal, maybe, he wouldn't be with thieves and rip-off men. 'What the fuck's normal anyway?' he asked himself.

Lost in thought, he paid no attention to the cigarette burning away, or to the hot ash falling on the seat; he imagined cool, air-conditioned libraries. The quiet pages of a book, poetry, music, songs. He hummed more of the song, a favourite of his grandmother's.

Carlos slid the car in an aquaplane movement, snapping Blackie out of his daydream.

'Where's that speed, fuck ya, Carlos? Let's have a line.'

Carlos fought hard to steady the car, and put it back on the straight and narrow, stammering, 'I … in, in, in the esky, brother. Want me to pull over?'

'Naa … keep going. Gittin sicka driving.'

Carlos smiled. He knew what Blackie was saying. Blackie reached for his knife and sliced off a bit of the filthy, white fury. As much as Blackie liked speed, he wouldn't use heroin. He never used the needle and the spoon for his business. He couldn't stand the thought of sticking himself. And he promised himself that he'd kill anyone who tried to coax him that way. He knew what he was doing. Carlos and Rips had trackmarks cut into the inside of their arms, but Blackie kept his arms clean from needles' prick marks.

Blackie quickly rinsed his mouth out with a hot, flat soft drink that was hours old.

'Fuck!' he said as he shook his head in disgust. 'Aww! That's fucked, man!' he yelled.

His tongue stung with the small ulcers that had developed from the battery acid or whatever it was that they cut the drug with. His teeth felt as sharp as razors and his bottom lip, full of scar tissue and red raw, was burning from the acidic shit.

Carlos looked to see if Blackie was going to offer him some more of that powerful stuff for all the hard driving he'd done. But he knew he'd better not ask after his fuck-up back at the shop. Blackie saw the subtle glances from the Spaniard as he swallowed hard. After a quick look over into the back seat – Rips was still sound asleep – he looked directly at the hungry Carlos.

''Ere! Fuck ya!' he said to the big-eyed driver.

The Spaniard nodded with a smile. Carlos would have been happy to be given just a point or maybe two if he was lucky. Blackie gave him heaps. There must have been at least half a gram, maybe more, stuck to the blade. Enough to blow Carlos away.

Carlos whispered, 'Thanks, Blackie.'

He watched as Blackie took another swallow, then saw where Blackie put the speed. Watched him place it back down there beneath the cans, down deep in the esky. A few specks fell on Carlos' trouser leg and the Spaniard did his best with a wet finger to get the last little bit into his hungry mouth. Blackie gave Carlos a smile and a nod, then looked away.

Blackie waited for the drug to make him forget. With

the window down, he drew a deep breath. The rushing air smelt clean and fresh. He looked towards the sky and noticed the clouds, dark, ready to drop their load.

'Sweeeeet summer rain!' he yelled at the rushing wind.

And then, as an afterthought, he screamed to the sky, 'Hey! All you farmer bastards! Fucken thieves! Git off my grandmother's country! And … Pay the rent!'

No one heard. Only his travelling mates and some magpies on a fence bore witness as the car rolled along.

The sudden rush of cool air woke Rips from his slumber.

Rips stretched and swore, 'Fuck me! Woz 'appenin, cuz?' he asked.

But, before Blackie could answer, Rips said, 'Pull over, man, wanna take a piss.'

Carlos eased the car onto the wet red gravel and brought it to a stop.

'Turn it off, man! I'm sicka fucken drivin. Let's have a rest for a while. If coppers come … Then let 'em come,' Blackie said. 'Wot yer reckon, Rips?' He turned. 'Stretch our legs, hey?'

He wanted to walk on his grandmother's country again, and that was that.

Big Rips, scratching his hairy belly, lazily, said, 'Yeah … Don't give a fuck, brother. I'm sicka dis back seat, man. Got smokes, Carlos?'

Rips jumped out of the back and made his way to a tree to piss. He pissed for such a long time that it made Blackie laugh out loud.

'What. You a fucken camel or something, boy? How much piss can a man have in 'im?'

Rips gave him a silly smile from over his shoulder and as he finished, he whinnied like a horse – long and loud! Then he said with that huge smile that covered his black face, 'Where's that smoke, big fulla?'

Carlos chucked him the packet of cigarettes and lighter. Rips lit a smoke and offered the packet to Blackie, as if they were his own.

He watched Blackie light his fag, walk away and then stop, looking out across the huge, almost-ready-to-harvest lucerne.

Blackie had things on his mind. He thought of the nursing home where he had left his dying grandmother. 'Fuck!' he said, wishing that he'd done things differently. He kicked the dirt hard.

He watched the lucerne heads bend and sway together in a natural dance as the wind blew through the crop. For a moment, he recalled the times when young girls in high school danced the Pride of Erin and the rumba with him. He remembered Yuko, the Japanese exchange student at the girls' school, who looked at him with a smile. She could dance better than all of them. She moved like a bird in silent flight, gliding perfectly across a dirty floor, making him feel like a beautiful dancer.

'Wonder what they'd all think of me now?' he asked himself, thinking about his decision to kill.

He looked away into the distance, away far off to the horizon. He wondered what was there, beyond … He thought about his grandmother out there. Dancing to clap sticks. Dancing and chanting. She'd make the dust fly with her feet on home soil.

He kicked his boots off and took his shirt off and stood barefooted on the wet ground. He carefully reached down, gathered mud, and painted his forehead and then, he painted his arms. He turned around and faced Rips and Carlos. Carlos' mouth fell open. And the cigarette fell onto his lap. Rips didn't know what to make of it. He just stood there, looking shamed.

Blackie began to chant a traditional chant. And then he began to dance. Muddy water flew up and wet his cheek. He bowed his head and held his arms wide, doing a dance like the eagle gliding in silent flight … He was dancing a warning.

'Huh!

Huh!

Huh!

Brrrrrrrrrrrrrrrrrrrrrrrrrr!

SSSSSSSSSSSssss!

Ahhhhhhhhhh!

Brrrrrrrrrrrr!

SSSSSSSSS.'

Carlos and Rips watched Blackie dancing his country back. Even the silly lucerne stood still and paid attention.

Blackie knew that whitefullas didn't know the dance he was doing. 'After tomorrow,' he told himself, 'they'll all know me name.'

He turned his mind to women again. He imagined those skinny white schoolgirls hiding their smiles behind their hands, not looking at him directly. He thought of his grandmother. His murdered mother – the woman whose face he couldn't remember. The woman murdered when she brought the wrong man home one night. The woman who gave him life, whose life was taken in white rage by a someone who was never pursued nor found. Blackie was two years old and was found the next day when his nan came to visit. He was screaming for mother's milk, standing in a pissy nappy next to his mother's bloody and broken body on the kitchen floor. And, he imagined the father he never met, a man with no face, shrouded in black. The man who fucked his young mother and told her to keep the evening light on for him and he'd be home after sunset. He never returned, she didn't see him again. Blackie grew up fatherless.

He imagined other black men. He imagined them black brothers, all right there with him! *RIGHT THERE!* Dancing the warrior dance with him. Bringing his grandmother's country back. He clapped his hands and chanted louder:

'Huh! Huh! Huh!
Brrrrrrrr!
SSSSSS!

Ahhhhhh!

Brrrrrrrr!'

He threw his head back in joy, trying to kiss the sky. His voice echoed back from the rocks. The country knew that a warrior had arrived to claim his place. He cut his foot. But he didn't feel it at all. The Wiradjuri warrior felt beautifully alive. Dancing. Dancing for the country. Dancing for his people. Dancing for his life.

The world fell silent around him. The bush and everything else watched on and admired his power. When he finished, he felt strong. He put his shoes and his shirt back on and turned and leant on the wire. Even the wire buzzed from his rhythm.

He went back to thinking of his grandmother, and the old woman in the shop, then what he wanted to do to McWilliams. He kicked his shoe deep into the soft soil in anger. He was kicking McWilliams to pieces. Memories of athletic carnivals, cricket games, of whistles and puffs of blue smoke as the starter's gun exploded, came rushing back as his eyes closed.

'No more silly games, copper!' he promised.

He felt his skin sticky from dancing, and felt himself full of warrior spirit.

Rips walked over to him, slowly. Rips had his head down, seemingly not knowing how to look at Blackie now that Blackie was painted in mud and dancing up war. Rips held out his hand and offered Blackie a rag from the back seat. Blackie took it and slopped it with water from a puddle on the ground, then wiped himself clean. Rips turned and walked away a little farther down the fence line, giving Blackie his space.

Meanwhile, Carlos watched the men slyly from inside the car. He chose what he thought was the best time to pinch a bit more while the black men did whatever it was that they were doing out there. He reached, without looking, and found the small satchel beneath the ice.

Carlos kept his eyes trained on his two companions; he smiled, as if there were nothing going on. His eyes searched for the slightest movement of shoulder, head, hip or leg that would indicate one of the boys was onto him. His heart thumped hard in his chest. Adrenaline surged through his body. His black hair stuck to his forehead. He felt dizzy. Sweat rolled down his forehead onto his nose.

'So far … So fucken good!' he whispered.

His nimble fingers prised open the satchel now in his lap. He pulled a little penknife from his shirt pocket and scraped a fair chunk from the decreasing stash. He swallowed the stuff immediately then dropped the knife back into his pocket in one fluid action.

He didn't mind the taste of the Force. No, Carlos loved it! Especially stolen fruit. He silently snapped the packet back together and quietly replaced it deep inside the esky … way down beneath the melting ice.

'Toooo easy, man!' he whispered, grinning a thief's smile. 'Who's stupid now, you fucks?'

He reckoned he'd look less suspicious if he was out of

the car when the blackfullas returned. So he snatched a beer, and by the time Blackie and Rips returned he was leaning casually on the bonnet, swigging grog, as innocent as a choir boy, feeling cool as a cucumber on steroids.

Blackie was way too lost in his own thoughts to see Carlos doing his stealing, and Rips was way too ashamed about watching Blackie's dancing to see either, and so Carlos got away with the theft. He heard Blackie say: 'Fuck 'em. Fuck reconciliation.'

A tree that Blackie stood near heard him swearing, but the tree decided not to say anything. It just stood there doing tree things – swaying, holding soil together, that kind of stuff. Keeping secret things secret.

Blackie continued to curse the world and himself.

'Fuck everything. And, FUCK ME TOO!' he swore at himself. 'Fuck me,' he repeated.

Blackie smoked a cigarette and looked at the dark sky. He knew they'd have to make a move if they were going to get to Dubbo before sundown. In Dubbo, he wanted one last big night out before the showdown with McWilliams. He watched the big clouds, dark, purple and grey:

She walks in beauty, like the night
of cloudless climes and starry skies …

He dedicated 'The Highwayman' to the sky above, too:

The wind was a torrent of darkness
among the gusty trees.

The moon was a ghostly galleon
tossed upon cloudy seas.
The road was a ribbon of moonlight over the purple moor,
And the highwayman came riding –
Riding – riding –

Listening from a few feet away, Rips piped up and said, 'Wot you talkin bout, Black?'

'Bout shit, bruz,' Blackie replied, smiling, not realising he'd been heard.

Rips laughed loud and slapped Blackie on the back. Blackie laughed too. Blackie's dark mood was lightened by the slap, causing both men to relax a little. They clinked their beer cans together in a celebration of their blackness.

Blackie quietly wondered what the original Wiradjuri people who owned that country, back before the arrival of the whitefullas, might have thought when they first saw the white ghosts in men's clothes. 'Terra nullius, man!' he yelled at the bush. 'Terror-shit!' he cried at the sky.

Rips laughed at Blackie's cry. It was more of a nervous laugh, recognising the moment, and joining in with Blackie.

'Ya right there, big fulla. Bet, what can we do? Deys call me a career crim, and you – you jest another wild blackfulla with chips on ya shoulder. Who's gonna fucken listen to us cunts?'

Blackie looked at Rips, smiled. And, then spat and threw his half-emptied beer can as hard as he could, and yelled, 'Fucken dogs!'

'Gee, dey must be fucken rich, those farmer pricks, hey Black? How much ya reckon all dass worth?' Rips asked. Rips swallowed a full mouthful of beer, burped loud, and shook his head in amazement.

'Dunno. More than me and you'll ever see in our lifetime, brother. That's for sure. Come on, let's git movin. Look at this up 'ere,' Blackie continued, pointing to the sky.

'I'm with you, big fulla,' Rips said. 'Come on Carlos, fuck ya. Less roll … Reb it up little boy. Let's ride!' Rips yelled.

Blackie heard the sound of thunder ringing across the mid-western sky. He looked at Rips and looked at the sky, saying, 'The drums of war are beatin, bruz, the drums of war. Watch yourself up 'ere, mate. Those cops are dogs! An, an, there's lota give-ups in Dubbo, bro.'

'Yeah, I know there are, bud. Never liked that 'ole,' Rips replied.

'Me neither,' Blackie agreed.

The first soft drops of rain splashed the windscreen as they drove away again towards Dubbo.

5

Down the Road

'Fuck, star … star … start'n feel crook, Black,' Rips complained, beginning to feel the ill effects of stale breath and an empty stomach.

'Well, that will hardly do, will it, ya fat bastard!' Blackie said, already searching for the speed. He found the drugs and offered it to Rips. 'Want some a dis?' he asked.

Overcome with joyous greed, 'Oh fuck! Yeah, man,' Rips replied.

He clapped his hands and leant forward to rest his arms on the back of Blackie's seat.

'Who ya git that off, Black?' Rips asked for future reference.

'Big Tamper owed. Gimme a eight ball,' Blackie answered.

'How come?' Rips inquired.

'I looked after his nephew at Silverwater,' Blackie answered quietly.

Blackie cut himself another slash from the speed, and offered the bag to Rips, who took a heap of it, and washed it down with his last swig of beer. He smiled a satisfied smile and passed the bag back to Blackie, knowing that soon he'd be flying high, flying away in a fast car. As raindrops hit the windscreen, streaking away to the bottom of the sill, Blackie wondered if his end was nigh. Carlos drove faster than before, as he was getting excited to be getting nearer to Dubbo and to rock 'n' roll. Blackie told him to slow down.

'If you kill me, Carlos,' he warned, 'Rips … You'll bust him if anything happen to me, ay bud?'

Rips loved taking the piss outa Carlos.

'Fucken oath I will, brother! Better wake up to yourself, Carlos!' the big man joked.

Carlos slowed the car a bit and trying to sound like the dude in Cheech and Chong's *Up in Smoke* said, 'What? Don't say you guys are afraid of a *leedle speed*, are you man?'

They drove through Wellington without any dramas. Blackie breathed a sigh of relief when they hit the Dubbo side of the town.

'Play this one for me, Rips?'

Effortlessly, Rips hit the C chord on his old guitar. Blackie was peaking, and broke into a song that he made up with Rips when they were in the can.

Um broke
I got no dough
Yeah I'm broke
Right down to my old broken toe
When ya got no money
Ya got no honey
And nowhere ta go

Uh, Oh. Uh Oh. Uh, Oh

Big Rips improvised a little riff that suited the bluesy nature of the song perfectly. Blackie continued:

One and one is two. And two and two is four

I'm sittin at the table

But you're walkin out the door

Yeah, I'm broke

Got no dough

When ya got no money

Ya got no honey

And nowhere to go

Rips slipped then into a darker mood. He began singing Zac Martin's 'Backroads', alone.

PART II

6

Dubbo, Dirty Old Town

Gradually, the rain eased. Blackie heard five bells ring out from a distant church. Turning into the Dubbo cemetery, the sound of the bells echoed all around. By the looks of the dirt road, now red mud, the rain had been falling for hours. The car slipped and slid all the way, right up to the end of the row that Blackie pointed out.

'Home,' he declared.

Carlos looked at him, 'This dump?'

Blackie smirked, 'Yeah, man. Love this place. Love every inch of it.'

Carlos shook his head, 'Whose country is this?'

'Wiradjuri. Dis all Wiradjuri land 'ere, man. Always was … Always will be, too!' Blackie answered.

Looking away, Blackie noticed another car, way over the other side of the cemetery. But Blackie didn't look long enough to recognise that the car was stuck in mud.

Inside that vehicle was a young woman, distraught and scared. In the baby seat slept her young baby, blowing little milky bubbles, unaffected by his mother's dilemma.

Carlos needed to take a piss, really bad. He jumped from the car as soon as he brought the V8 to a standstill.

Blackie was caught by surprise and disgusted when he realised.

'Hey! What ya think ya doin man? You fuck off and go over there to the fucken toilet and do that! My grandmother's buried here!'

Blackie flew out of the car. He moved towards Carlos with such speed that Carlos slipped over. Blackie threw his can of beer at Carlos. The can missed Carlos by inches and Carlos scurried out of Blackie's reach.

'Sa … Sa … Sorry brother! Don' hit me, bra. I didn't know, bra …' Carlos cried.

Blackie couldn't reach the Spaniard to punch him, so he continued to hurl abuse across the cemetery.

'Fucken kill you, you bastard!' Blackie yelled.

Blackie watched Carlos race across the wet ground, slipping and falling in his haste to escape a bashing.

'Ya dirty bastard, Carlos!' Blackie screamed.

'He, he, he's fucken mad, that bastard!' Carlos cursed to himself.

In the back seat of the car, Rips pretended not to see what had happened. But he was struggling to hold back his laughter watching the fleeing Carlos.

'Fucken idiots!' he whispered, pretending to cough uncontrollably. His eyes filled with tears of joy, and he shook his head when Blackie turned to him.

'See that, Rips? No fucken respect, that little bastard! Fucken kill 'im when he comes back. Don't they know *anything* bout sacred sites? Silly bastards?'

Big Rips tried to look concerned for his mate, and, sensing that Blackie already was beginning to cool down from the blow-up, said, 'Yeaaah! ... Dey silly right, brother. Don't worry bout it, man. He, he don't know any better, mate. Don't hit 'im ... we might need 'im later.'

Rips knew how to calm Blackie down. Blackie's rage would always quickly evaporate, and in a short while, he wouldn't be bothered with talking about Carlos anymore. He settled back on the front seat of the car, wanting another line of speed. Rips could see that Blackie was flying high. He reckoned that if he played the understanding and best-mate guy, Blackie would soften, and probably share more of the speed.

'He's fucken lucky you're 'ere, brother!'

Rips quickly jumped on the opportunity. 'Big Rips the man for dem silly fullas, bra. Leave 'im to me. You got important business 'ere! You gotta talk to old Aunt out there, 'steada being fucked round with a silly cunt like 'im.'

Blackie agreed that Rips was correct on the matter and decided to take more speed.

'Fuck the world, man,' he said as he fished in the bottom of the esky for the drugs.

Rips nodded and continued strumming the guitar.

Hungry for more drugs also, Rips asked, 'Where's dat gas, bra?'

Blackie brought the small satchel out from its icy place and held it up for Rips to see.

''Ere big fulla. Ab some a dis!' he offered.

Blackie had his knife out. His hands were shaking too much to cut an equal amount for both. But he eventually had what looked to be three or four points, and offered them to Rips.

Big Rips nearly swallowed the whole blade as his mouth enveloped the steel to suck the speed clean from it in one gulp. He sucked the blade a second, and then a third time, just to make sure he got every last speck that was there. He swallowed and winced at the taste of the drug then polished off the half a can of beer to wash it down. Rips burped, shook his head and watched as Blackie swallowed what looked to be twice the amount.

Blackie went through his routine again, 'Aww, that's fucked, man. Fuck, I hate the taste of that shit.'

He tightly secured the satchel, but this time wrapped it snugly in a dirty handkerchief he fished from his jeans pocket, and then placed it deep inside his shirt pocket.

'Ay, ta, ta tanks, my little bra!' the grateful Rips said.

'No worries, son. Rips, I gotta go out 'ere, brother. Wanna talk to me nan. Jump in the front, bud, and play this one and turn it up loud man! Her favourite it was,'

Blackie handed Rips an old country CD that his nan had given him years ago for his birthday. He looked so deep into Rips' eyes that the big fulla got the message that he wanted to be left alone whilst he spoke to his grandmother's spirit.

Rips understood that Blackie was wasted and nodded an acknowledgement. 'I'll fucken keep that bastard 'ere with me, when he comes back, bra. Hey, he's been gorn for a while, Black. Don't tink he fucked off, do ya?' Rips said.

'Hope not,' Blackie said softly.

Thinking about Carlos, Blackie became pissed off again.

He got out of the car and moved towards the unkempt grave of his grandmother.

A sorrowful wind had crept up from across the flat plain and wrapped itself around Blackie. Filled with speed and grog and emptiness he stared at the grave and felt the soft coolness of the wind on his face. Standing crooked like his old mate Crusoe stood bent, out of shape, in his raggedy clothes looking like a scrubby hobo, his face wet from tears.

'G'day, Nan,' he breathed.

He quieted himself, closing his eyes and imagining her standing in front of him. Everything else around him faded in the dark. He couldn't hear the wind or the music or anything. He stood in a clouded space in an afterworld place. Slowly her ghost appeared. He smiled, and she smiled, and they spoke to each other from another place – a silent place, in silence together. 'My boy, my boy, my beautiful black boy,' he heard her say. Tiredness had him unsteady on his feet.

'Aww, Nan!' he murmured.

He carefully sat on the grave next to his grandmother's, straightening himself before he spoke with her ghost again, about the business of McWilliams. He asked her for permission to go to war. But he knew that she would never support that. He saw her smiling, shaking her head, warning him. He sat back and leant on the headstone, taking in evening for ten long minutes. Smoking as he sat, he began to worry. He stood up and walked back to the car.

Deftly strumming the guitar, Rips was surprised when he looked up to see Blackie appear at the door.

'Waa … waa … whatcha finished, brother?' Rips blurted out.

Blackie knew that his returning to the car had spooked Rips from the way Rips scrunched his knees up and pushed himself hard into the seat.

'Naa. Not yet. Need a charge. Pass us one,' Blackie asked softly.

Blackie's eyes were peeled. He looked across the cemetery towards the car he'd seen on the way in. He was looking for that Carlos.

'Where's that idiot?' Blackie asked as he took the beer from Rips' hand. 'Keep an eye out for him, man. I want that bastard to drive.'

'No worries, man,' Rips said.

Blackie spun on his heels, and without speaking again, headed back to the grave. In the fading light he struggled to see his grandmother's name on the cross. He scrubbed it with a spitty thumb but still couldn't make out the letters.

The wind blew up stronger as he stood and sipped his beer, peering into space. The wind blew him around, tossing his untidiness from side to side. It pushed him forwards and pulled him backwards. But mostly, it pushed him towards the west. He thought about old stories told to him by old people …

'The wind is the message carrier. Be still. Be quiet. You'll hear.'

He tossed his beer far away, off into the spare paddock. He straightened up. Standing as tall as his legs would hold him, he closed his eyes and tried to open his imagination up to the wild wind. McWilliams' name came. He knew he'd meet him soon. The message was there, plain and clear. It came to him on the wind.

In the toilet block on the other side of the cemetery, Carlos washed his hands and then his face.

He looked closely, smiled and admired his thin face. He ran wet fingers through his thick, black hair, flicking a few loose strands so as to make them look casual and unintended, uncombed – kind of natural-looking. With the Force surging through his body, he felt so alive, so excited. He gave a low wolf whistle, winked at his reflection, then turned on the balls of his feet and walked out of the toilet block.

Outside, Carlos closed his eyes and drew a deep breath. He threw his head back and stretched his arms, neck and shoulders as he let out a long sigh, 'Fuck I'm horny!'

He was surprised by a young woman, with the baby in her arms, only a few feet away from him.

'Sorry, car's stuck in the mud over there. Reckon you could help me?' she said. 'I can't git any mobile coverage out here otherwise I would have rung my dad.'

Carlos quickly adjusted to the situation, summing up the look of the woman in an instant.

Experience told him she was still breastfeeding. Late teens, maybe twenty at the most, he thought. Bosom was plump and full. 'Nice tits,' he told himself.

'Uh huh. Let's have a look, ay?' said Carlos.

He allowed the woman to take the lead back to her car, hoping he might be able to see through the thin cotton material and get a good look at her arse, or at least her underpants.

The woman's dress was tight on her body. She was aware that the man was eyeing her off but there was not much she could do about the situation she found herself in. She knew the danger she was in. She slowed so that Carlos walked beside her so that he would not be getting an eyeful of her from behind.

'It's just over here,' she said. 'I'm Silvia. This is my baby, Jimmy,' she said, kissing her young child lightly on the cheek.

'G'day. I'm Carlos,' Carlos replied.

Carlos kept sneaking quick peeks at her cleavage. Aware that she might catch him perving, he made his glances as occasional and inconspicuous as possible. She started drawing the baby closer to cover herself up.

Realising she'd caught him out, he flashed her what he thought was his prettiest smile, then hastened to explain.

'Sa, sa, sorry Silvia. I, I, I know it's rude ta stare, ba, ba, but you remind me of someone I know. You haven't been on tele, 'ave ya?'

She looked like she knew he was bullshitting her, but recognised the funny side of the whole event so she decided to let him off the hook and instead of telling him off right there and then, she said, 'Ha! Me? Not likely, mate!'

She threw her head back and scoffed. Her laughter was a pleasant change from the harsh language and country music that Carlos had been suffering most of the long trip to this place.

'Not out here in this rathole, anyhow,' she went on to say.

Silvia's family came to live in Dubbo when her father took up the manager's position at the local oil company depot. He loved being king of the bush, but she longed for the bright lights of Sydney. Dubbo was hell to her. First, there was the death of her mother two years ago from the cancer. Then, she got pregnant to Springer – the footballer. Springer took off to Sydney on a football contract, leaving her and baby to look after themselves. A short note saying she should 'get over' him and 'move on'.

He said, 'I'd be no good as a father anyway, and you're way too good for me.'

There were no hugs and kisses. She screamed his name as loud as she could, and yelled out of her bedroom window that he was a good-for-nothing, chicken-livered, cock-sucking bastard. She cursed and hoped he'd die a thousand times, a thousand different ways.

There was never any time for her these days and she quickly grew out of her schoolgirl ways when her baby came.

'Oh … Coulda swore I saw you on tele.'

'Piss off!'

Her little car was stuck up to the back axle in the greasy, red mud.

Carlos wasn't stepping off the dry surface of the road in his two-hundred-dollar Julius Marlow imported leather shoes for no one. He bent low and looked at the car from the road to confirm that it was indeed bogged, 'Well … there's ya problem right there! Got a towrope?'

They laughed together, and Silvia said, 'Yeah. Got all that stuff in the boot.'

They walked the long road around back to where the black men were. The wind dropped, and the resident crows fled to their resting places for the evening. The cemetery gave Carlos the creeps. He didn't understand the fascination that the blacks had with the dead anyway. It reminded him of his superstitious mother and her love of Jesus and all that crap. Feeling he was being watched made him jumpy and had him walking fast to get away from the dark and back to the light of the car and the company of men. Silvia struggled to keep up, but noticed Carlos' change in mood.

'Don't tell me that you're scared of ghosts?' Silvia asked.

'Wha, wha, what make ya say that?' Carlos retorted, surprised.

'Hey, s'alright. Ya just look like ya a bit windy that's all. Lookin round all the time.' She laughed as she waved her free arm in a wide arc to indicate the whole of the cemetery, 'Not the dead ya have ta worry bout, as my mum useda say.' Silvia laughed.

Rips was lying back, feet dangling outa the doorway. The music coming from the car stereo was loud and country. Buck Owens and his Buckaroos were singing 'In the Palm of Your Hand'. The sound filled the empty space of the early evening, waking the baby.

Cradling her baby close she whispered, 'Hello, my baby! You just wake up? You've had a big sleep.'

Jimmy felt soft and warm to her touch. She went through all the immediate checks with the baby. Knowing that he'd be ready for a feed, she wanted to get away to home as quickly as possible. 'We'll be home soon,' she assured her baby with soft kisses.

Jimmy settled back into the safety and comfort of his mother's bosom, and as quickly as he had woken, he closed his eyes and drifted back to sleep.

Hearing the baby gurgle made Carlos ask, 'Kid alright, hey?'

She tightened the light baby blanket around Jimmy and when satisfied the child was all snug and secure, and re-gripping the hidden screwdriver, she said, 'He's fine! Reckon you can get these blokes to help, or what? It's dark now and I wanna get him home outa the night air. Now!' she whispered urgently.

Her tone caught Carlos by surprise and deflated his enthusiasm in a flash. Those sparkling eyes of hers, that had so impressed him a few minutes before, now flashed as wild as lightning in the darkened sky.

Hearing Silvia and Carlos, Rips looked up surprised in seeing the attractive woman with the baby in her arms standing next to Carlos.

'Took ya fucken time, didn't ya, Carlos? Whatcha walk all the way ta town ta do a shit, or what? He been lookin for you, man!' he said, nodding towards the direction of Blackie.

Rips eyed Silvia carefully, and before Carlos could answer, he acknowledged Silvia by way of a nod.

She nodded back towards the big black man in the car.

She lowered her head towards Rips and she gently kissed her baby's head. But her eyes didn't leave Rips – not even for a second. He frightened her. She thought that he could see right through her and that he knew that she was terrified of him.

Rips had that look of hungry lust written all over his ugliness, like he just wanted to fuck her senseless and leave her for dead in the mud.

She looked towards where Rips had nodded his head. She strained to make out the shape of someone sitting alone on a granite gravestone.

Carlos was scared to hear Blackie had inquired about his whereabouts.

'Her car's stuck in the mud over there,' Carlos said, pointing. 'She, sh, she's got a towrope an all. Wanna know if we'll help her git it out cause she's gotta git her baby home.'

Rips was not listening to the squirming Carlos. He was interested in Silvia and enjoyed her vulnerability, which had him feeling powerful and horny.

'Nice name that, Silvia,' he said.

The speed had reignited his need for sex, and his focus was her. 'Wanna fuck ya! Wanna fuck ya! Wanna fuck ya …' he repeated to himself.

Rips sniffed the air in the faint hope that he might get a whiff of her. He imagined his tongue on her skin. Images of gaol sex crept into his thoughts. He imagined that he could still smell the sweat of the scared men struggling against his weight and against his hand held over their mouths as their souls screamed for mercy. The more they tried to scream, the higher the thrill. He had grown to like it. Rips had stopped thinking about morals years ago, wasting away in that bastard, sandstone hell that's known as Bathurst gaol. A couple of the other boys told him that it was okay. That's what they all do when they're inside. It didn't mean that he'd become a poofter. So it didn't take long for him to love any hole in the dark. But as much as Rips enjoyed having his way with those tight young boy arses, hearing them cry and begging him to stop, nothing satisfied him like a woman could.

'Well, ya better go an ask him. He's over there, doin business,' Rips said, casually nodding towards Blackie.

Silvia didn't hang around to be told again. She didn't hesitate a second longer and briskly walked towards the man at the grave.

Sweat ran down her chest and hung around her eyes. She approached the man near the grave, stopping a few feet away, watching him for a brief moment, seeing him rock gently back and forwards with his arms around his legs. She stood close enough to hear him chanting something Aboriginal.

Na, naa naa. Yumm-ma naa-numm-naa. Yumm-ma naa, numm naa.

Na, naa naa. Yumm-ma naa-numm-naa. Yumm-ma naa, numm naa …

She listened for a short while summoning the strength her body could muster, then said, 'Hi, mate …'

Blackie reeled and fell. He ended up with his arse in the mud.

'Waa! What? Who are ya?' he stammered.

Blackie's eyes were red and sore. He strained to make out who was the figure of the woman in the dark that had spoken aloud to him.

'Got me baby here with me. My name's Silvia. Car's stuck over there,' she replied, pointing, trying to get all the information out in one purge.

Blackie looked towards where she pointed and scrambled to his feet. He straightened himself up, trying to strike a more dignified pose. Cold sweat ran down his face. His palms were wet from sweat too. His bones ached.

Silvia watched him scramble and slip on the slippery ground.

⋆

Blackie stared at her staring at him.

Long seconds separated them, just for a few seconds.

Unsure what to do next, Silvia went to draw away. She watched him raise his hand in an indication for her to stand still.

Blackie stepped up to her, looking deep into her as if he was seeing right through. 'Nan?' he whispered.

Blackie looked harder still, searching to see his grandmother in Silvia's face. He walked towards Silvia, reaching out to hold her.

Silvia gripped her baby tight in one arm and pushed Blackie away with the other. He slipped arse over head.

He hit the ground with a jolt. The fall shocked him and brought him to his senses.

'Ahh … Sorry sis. I thought … I, I, I. Didn't mean nothing,' he apologised.

Not knowing what the correct thing to do was, Silvia stood stock-still. She wanted to run but found that her feet were stuck fast and hard with the mud. No matter how hard she tried, she could neither move nor speak. Her lungs felt like they were going to burst and her throat tightened to the point where she thought she'd pass out from lack of oxygen, but still she couldn't move or speak.

★

It took Blackie more seconds to gather himself before he said, 'Huh? What ya want? Wad ya say?' he continued.

They both watched each other, looking for some way to speak to the other.

Finally it was Silvia that spoke again. 'Me car – bloody thing slid off the road in the rain. It's stuck. Can ya give me a hand?' she asked.

She waited a few seconds and then offered, 'Got a couple a dollars, that's all, if ya help me?'

'Naa. No need for that, sista. The boys and me have ya out there and on ya way in a minute. Woz ya name there? Woz that little fulla ya got in ya arms there?' Blackie said, forgetting that Silvia had already told him her name.

She thought that there was something different about this man. Though he stared at her twice, he did not have that predator hunger that Carlos and Rips had when they looked at her.

'Silvia's my name, and this is my baby, Jimmy,' she replied and lessened the tight grip on the screwdriver she held under the blanket.

Before he walked away with Silvia, he stood still and closed his eyes. He took a deep breath to fill his lungs full of the cemetery smell. He filled himself full of his grandmother's spirit. He looked for, and found, the candle, broken in the mud. He picked it up and walked to the head of his nan's grave and gently placed it next to the faded letters of love. He held two fingers to his lips and then ran those fingers across where once was painted his grandmother's name, her date of birth and the date of her death. Nan's ghost began to fade slowly away into the dark. Blackie reached into thin air. 'Don't leave,' he whispered. But the moment was gone, the ghost had disappeared, the smell of jasmine was everywhere, but his nan's image was gone. Silvia saw Blackie and then seemed to know what he was doing. She turned herself and her baby away from the scene, giving Blackie privacy.

Blackie picked up his small bag from the gravestone. He softened and became filled with wonder at the sight of the sleeping baby.

'Hey! He's a beauty, sis. How old, ay?' Blackie asked softly.

And on that cheek and o'er that brow
So soft, so calm, yet eloquent

Silvia blushed.

'C'mon. Let's git ya car outa here. Must be past the little Boorie's bedtime, ay? You from Dubbo?' Blackie said as they moved towards the car.

Silvia was caught off guard by the forthrightness of the stranger's demeanour. Sounding surprised and happy, she said, 'Yeah, I live here. Bet I'm originally from Sydney. What bout you?' she answered.

'Me? I'm from all over the place. Nowhere particular.'

As they walked the short distance back to the car, Silvia asked, 'What's your name, there, mate?'

'Blackie, sis. Jest call me Blackie,' he said.

Blackie got his travelling companions to assist, and in no time at all, they had Silvia's car back on the road.

Driving away, Silvia saw the strange trio fade from her view through her rear-view mirror. Something told her she'd see them again.

7

Love in a Dingy Bar

The wind blew in strong gusts making even the lampposts sway in the early evening.

The streets were mostly empty as the men drove. It was as if all those streets were theirs. House lights lit up the dirty yards and anything that wasn't tied down was flying around and up and down.

Dubbo is a city where people mostly live on double blocks of land. The large yards give the home owners space to grow gardens and vegetable patches. All alone to face the night, the rose bushes bent against the wind. The wind blew so strong that the leaves were blown right off the branches. So strong was the wind that even the stray dogs scurried to look for cover. The men drove slowly, making their way towards the centre of town, being rocked in the car by the wind and music and drugs and beer.

Recognising a skinny, hunched white man shuffling along the street, Blackie said, 'Hey, hey! Pull over, Carlos! Stop the car – I know dat bloke!'

★

Carlos eased the car to the kerb and brought it to a stop just behind the man. Blackie's window was open and he casually called, 'Hey! You there! Stop! This is the police!'

The skinny whitefulla froze in his tracks. He turned around slowly to find, leaning with his arm on the window frame of the car, his old friend Blackie.

'Should see your face, Fingers,' Blackie laughed aloud.

Feeling relieved and slightly shamed at the same time, the skinny man replied with a comment and a question to Blackie.

'Ya bastard! What the fuck ya doin 'ere?'

Fingers gathered himself and visibly beamed with happiness that it was not the police demanding him to stop. Blackie told him to 'Git in', asking Rips to move over to allow Fingers room to join them. Carlos put the car into drive, and then they slowly cruised down Lonely Street.

'Hey bud, dat's Rips, and dis 'ere's Carlos,' Blackie said, pointing to both of his travelling companions in turn.

Blackie was always short on introductions. But there wasn't any need for detailed explanations; the fact that he knew Fingers was good enough.

'How ya goin there, bud? Woz ya name again? Fingers?' Rips asked. He shook Fingers vigorously by the hand, offering him a swig from his beer.

⋆

Fingers took the beer and took a mouthful greedily. He liked the tone of the big man straight off the bat.

'Yeah, that's me name,' Fingers answered. 'Gee, you blokes must be desperate travellin round with this bloke!' he continued, pushing Blackie on the shoulder hard enough that Blackie hit his head against the windshield.

Glad to see his mate again, Blackie laughed. 'Look out, ya skinny bastard!'

'Hey! Still with ya woman? How's me big cousin Dorothy goin these days?' Blackie asked, turning to look at the expression on Fingers' face.

Fingers responded immediately. 'Wozza matter with *you*, Black? You know I'll never leave her!' he said.

Blackie roared with laughter. He laughed so hard he thought he'd piss himself. Blackie hadn't seen two people more devoted to each other than Fingers and Dot – 'Joined at the lips, and joined at the hips,' he joked about them, laughing loudly.

Not knowing any background to Fingers or the woman named Dorothy that Blackie had mentioned, Carlos and Rips stared at Blackie with blank looks upon their faces, wondering what was so funny. Blackie laughed so hard that he felt himself beginning to choke. He coughed and spluttered and swore as he tried to control himself.

Eventually, Blackie caught his breath, and recovered just long enough to recognise that the other men remained clueless to what had him in a fit of laughter. Blackie roared again, slapping the seat with his hand. Seeing this, the other men nervously joined in. Just a kind of giggle at first, but then the stupidity of the moment had them full tilt. They laughed all the way into Main Street.

The street was empty of people. Dust blew against the panes of glass, scratching away at telegraph poles and paper posters. The whole thing looked like a scene from a modern-day spaghetti Western – all it needed to complete the picture, was the whistling overture from Sergio Leone's *The Good, the Bad and the Ugly.*

When Blackie told Carlos to park the car, the mood changed to a deeper thing. He gave the street a quick look over, checking out who was who, and where whoever they were, were. He scanned the street looking for people in blue, remembering the cops back in Katoomba doing the same thing. He gave Rips a quick glance and raised an eyebrow in question to check if he had noticed anyone of suspicion that might be the law. Rips returned the look and, seemingly satisfied that he couldn't spy any police either, smiled a crooked smile. Without a word being spoken between the two, Blackie opened the door, and stepped out onto the street, feeling strong, fearless, and frightfully fucken lucky.

On the corner of Main Street and Talbragar, a singer played tambourine while the Salvation Army band played 'Life in a Northern Town'.

On the lookout for easy meat, Carlos whispered to Rips as they neared the entrance of the pub, 'Hey, this looks right,

Rips? Whaddya reckon? We score here for sure, brother!'

Blackie knew his comment was an attempt to hide his own deviance by coaxing Rips into it.

Small groups and couples stood leaning on the pub wall with their heads turned towards the inside, attempting to keep their talk secret. Their eyes flashed bright, quick as black cats, as Blackie's group passed. But the Dubbo crowd did not say 'g'day' or make any attempt at being friendly.

As Blackie pushed the heavy doors apart, the smell of stinking sweat and dirty people hit him like a punch in the face. The smell stung his eyes.

'Faaarrrk me!' Fingers exclaimed as the full smell of the stinking bar room hit him.

Blackie looked over his shoulder to Fingers and laughed.

As they walked into the bar, Blackie saw in a darkened corner four young guys deeply involved in young guys' business. They stood with their pants hanging down around their arses, wearing hoodies, trying to look dark and dangerous – trying to look gangsta style. Blackie gave them a nod and a smile of hello, remembering that everyone was young once, but they just looked, then looked away from him without a smile. Laughing at them, he softly whispered: 'Amateurs!'

To their right, a young woman, who looked to be little more than sixteen years old, sat breastfeeding her baby. Between puffs of her cigarette, and as drunks staggered round her, and despite a singer singing 'The Last Cheater's Waltz', she quietly sang to her baby – 'You're my little Aborigineeeee.'

Walking through the crowd, Carlos' eyes were everywhere and although there seemed to be standing room only, his keen eyes spotted a table near a window that'd give them perfect view of the street, and their car. 'Here boys!' he said.

As he went to sit, Carlos looked at the young Koori woman feeding her baby. 'See the size of her tit, man,' he whispered to Rips.

Rips was looking at the young mother too and nodding his head as a way of hello, but making no effort to make eye contact with her, in case it invited conversation or fight. Like Blackie he seemed to know that if she was out tonight, she must be really desperate. It was one of *those* nights. One of those crazy old nights that the men walked straight into, face-first.

'You're a good'n'alright, you cringer, Carlos ... See, Rips? Who said he was no good, Rips?' Blackie said, referring to Carlos.

Before Rips could respond, Carlos started begging Blackie. 'Pleeease! Don't call me that, Blackie! I don't want all these fellas thinkin I'm easy or somefin.'

Blackie had caught the whisper and seen the look Carlos made concerning the young Koori woman and scoffed, 'Cheap, easy and dirty, you, Carlos ... You fucker.'

*

Rips was oblivious. He let out a big cooee to inform all and sundry that he was back in town, and ready for fun.

Blackie looked at Rips and smiled and said to Rips, 'So much for keepin our heads down, ya silly bastard!'

There's comfort in a crowd, and Blackie knew that he had the collective weight of other blacks in the bar. Should coppers try to take him while there, they would have to face the crowd also. If they wanted to throw their weight around inside that stinking pub, they'd better put their boxing gloves on and be prepared to fight. So in the meantime, Blackie felt safe. Seated at the table, Rips stuck his hairy paw deep into his jeans pocket and withdrew it with two fifties, a ten and a few twenty-dollar notes.

'Hey, you fullas! Look what old Rips got! Where the fuck did dis come from?' he asked his mates.

Blackie was fast out of the blocks, replied, 'That's my money, bud. I stuck it in ya jeans back dere, past Penrith somewhere, cause me jeans got holes in 'em! See?'

Blackie turned his jeans pockets inside out and sure enough, they were like the way he felt – ripped and torn.

'Ahh! Fuck! Tort I was rich dere for minute, bud. La, la, let me shout youse all a drink, anyway!' he laughed. And before Blackie could stop him, Rips dragged Carlos out of his seat, and together they were off to the bar, full of hope and happiness.

Blackie laughed at his old mate, but watched him closely as he made his way to the bar, just in case Rips thought of making a sly detour towards the poker machine room. Blackie hated the misery that came from being broke all the time, and he hated the poker machines. Blackie looked at Fingers and said, 'Watch old mate there, bud … he's jest likely go spend the lot on the pokies before ya git up to do a piss. Bad gambler, that fulla mate.'

Fingers nodded, agreeing in the moment that he'd keep the thought in mind.

'Seem ta remember you useda like 'em too, hey Black? What happened?' Fingers asked.

'Jest got sicka givin all me dough to them hollo-neck bastards and never gittin anything back, that's all. Anyway, my old friend, what you been up to? Woz Dubbo like these days? Still the same old shithole as always?' Blackie asked, swaying unsteadily in his chair as the sound of music roared again.

He reached for the pack of cigarettes on the table and slipped, knocking the big glass ashtray to the floor. He recovered it and returned to his seat, let out a low growl and drew a deep breath of the smoke-filled air.

'Ya right, bro?' Fingers asked, reaching and laying a reassuring hand on Blackie's. 'Yeah, it's still the same shithole, still pushin blacks around. Still too many cops pushin their weight … All bout small business here, Black,' Fingers answered.

'Yeah, figured,' was Blackie's reply.

Blackie blinked and shook his head. He caught sight of the worried look on Fingers' face, and thought he could see Carlos in the distance with his hands full of drinks.

'Course I'm fucken right! You know me, brother! Blackfullas, always alright!' he laughed.

'Hey, who useda always say that? "I'm always right!" … JK, thas right …? Remember him Fingers, JK? He was a funny one, that fulla, hey?' Blackie went on.

JK the fighter, Blackie's uncle, always at war with the law and never a man to give in in a fight. JK would go down swinging. Two things he could do well was fight, and drink. And, Blackie missed him.

Blackie looked around the bar room. He looked from table to table and from the floor to the ceiling, at nothing in particular.

'Ya know,' he declared. 'I hate the smell in here … But I love the lights – I love the shadows.' He looked from corner to dark corner, taking in the shapes and things that hung around like bloodstains on a boxer's towel.

'Why ya say that, Black?' Fingers replied.

Blackie thought of shitty things he'd done – broken promises, lies he'd told, letters he'd never replied to. Thought of his chances and things he had pissed away into Nothing-ville.

Fingers was remembering JK and roused on Blackie, saying, 'Yeah. Course I remember JK. He stayed at our place often enough. What's the matter with you? You gone mad, or what?'

Blackie laughed and shook his head. 'Sorry man, I'm wrecked, bruz. Off me head, man.'

Fingers scratched and said, 'I seen the old fulla a couple a months ago. He came through here with one of his sons – Robert, I think … Was takin him down to Bathurst for court, or something. Said he was shacked up with a woman from Wilcannia, livin somewhere. Fucked if I know.'

'No shit hey?' Blackie declared. 'Bastard still kickin? Well, I'll be … Coulda swore he woulda met his maker by this time …'

Settling into a casual yarn, Blackie told Fingers about the swans fighting back at Katoomba.

'Hope we don't git into a blue here, mate,' Fingers said quietly.

Fingers knew that Blackie was off his head before they walked in. He did not need Blackie to tell him how things were. Fingers knew from the staggering and the scattering of Blackie that he was on a bender.

They kept the conversation on the light side, reminiscing for a short while, just filling in time until Rips and Carlos returned.

'Know what the whitefullas call that place – Wilcannia?' Blackie laughed. 'They say, Will-Kill-Ya! Hope old JK don't kill anyone down that way.'

Fingers failed to see what was funny about that. He'd been clipped once before by a Koori bloke from Wilcannia, thus he did not join in the laughter.

★

Blackie was letting his mind relax and recalled the time Fingers and Dorothy first met in Sydney. 'Hey bud, remember that weekend on the big Knockout in Sydney? The year they split it tween Mascot and Marrickville?' he asked.

Fingers smiled at Blackie. Fingers had been through this routine with Blackie before and he knew what was coming next. Blackie would often bring up the funny side of the lovemaking antics of Fingers and Dorothy, just for a laugh, whenever they got together. But Fingers played along.

'Naa, Blackie. What happened?' Fingers lied.

'That was a wild weekend, that one, Fingers – when big Dot first got with you. "Hey white boy! Come here … I'm 'Dot with the lot' … And you jest what I been lookin for!"' Blackie said, mimicking Dot.

Blackie laughed, and Fingers cringed. Fingers rolled his eyes and tried to look away. But Blackie just laughed louder at seeing Fingers squirm.

What had happened was that, during that weekend in Sydney, Fingers met Dot, and while people may have been sleepless in Seattle, in Redfern, Fingers – the thin man, and Dot – the big woman, tried fucking each other on the back seat of her red Holden Commodore. Fingers' lily-white arse was moving so fast in the urgent struggle for sexual relief that for a short while there, Blackie gave him the nickname 'The Blur'.

'Eleven years ago, Blackie. Our eldest boy was conceived in that back seat of the old car, that weekend. Eleven years ago. And ... you went round tellin everybody ta call me "The Blur", ya bastard! Didn't ya, hey?' Fingers laughed.

In equal good humour, Blackie denied the accusation as quickly as it was said, but both knew it was the Blackman who'd spread the yarn of 'Dot with the lot' and 'The Blur'.

'Tell ya what, old mate, if I didn't like ya, I'd make a movie about ya and me cousin and call it that ... "True Life Adventures of 'Dot with the Lot' versus 'The Kiwi Wonder – The Blur'"! Or "Blurring"!' Blackie laughed.

Rips and Carlos returned to the table with a round of beers. Rips had a Koori woman with him who walked a couple of steps behind the two men.

Rips had a peculiar inquiring look upon his face.

'Ya, ya fucken liar, Blackie!' were the first words he spoke.

Blackie didn't even bother to look up at him, but instead gave a broad grin and shook his head as he said, 'Bloody took ya long nuff ta work it out didn't it, ya big Murri?'

Blackie took a long swig of the cold beer.

'What's goin on?' Fingers inquired, looking confused.

Rips took control and invited the woman to join them as everybody moved to make space for her at the table. As Rips reached for a cigarette for himself, then offered the woman a smoke, he began to explain.

'Daz not your money, Blackie, ya big gee-wiz! Jest membered, I, I, I got fucken paid 'fore we … strike me dead, Fingers, ah! Ya gotta watch this one … He, he, he'd fucken tell ya water run uphill!'

Blackie knew that Rips would have figured the truth out, sooner or later, and that it was only a joke that Blackie'd played.

'Anyway, bud … how bout a loan till I git paid, hey? Ya must have a sly fifty there for your old mate Blackie, ay? Seein that you the big captain,' Blackie said, laughing.

'Captain fucken Cook! Fuck you. But, never mind bout dat now,' Rips said, changing the subject. He half turned to the woman and said, 'Wanna inna-duce you all to diz lubly lady, 'ere,' deliberately over-exaggerating the woman's importance in a gesture of good humour and respect. Trying to sound like he was a host on a crummy television game show he said:

'Let me inna-duce youse to dis 'ere ravin beauty. She's known throughout the west as Darlin Riba Queen! That's right folks – don't muck round with her, cause she's all the way from dat beautiful town-a Bourke … crows fly backwards – all dat shit. Where men are men, and sheep are scarce cause all Blackie's mob ate 'em out. Name's Tegan and she comes with a reputation as a singer and a dancer. And she's best-lookin woman 'ere, thas for sure!' he said, smiling.

He pretended to joke with her by burying his face into the crook of her neck, being sure that he was taking in a sly feel of her curves. She felt his moves, but didn't push him away.

They all erupted in rowdy laughter at Rips.

'You're a spinner!' she roused.

She slapped him on the arm.

He pretended that it hurt and that he was wounded. Then, to over-emphasise chivalry, he drew her chair out and assisted her to sit, trying to be Prince Charming.

'See it's true, bud ...' Rips said to Blackie. 'A rose can bloom in the desert.'

But Tegan did not pay attention to Rips' comment. She was more interested in Blackie. She thought she recognised his face, but was not certain. She wondered if he was her cousin. 'Ya name's Blackie, tain't it?' she asked him.

Blackie watched her relax into a chair opposite himself, wondering who she was.

He stared at her in an attempt that he might recognise a familiar family trait of one of his countrymen. But there was nothing there that he could place her with. And with that, he had no idea if she was a relative of his, or not.

Having been away from home for such a long time, he was not sure as to who were friends or relations or enemies anymore. Best, he thought, was to respect and make friends with her, and to treat her as if she was a relative. Regardless, he knew that come tomorrow night, everyone in the old, dusty former frontier town of Bourke would know that he was in Dubbo in a sad and sorry state wrecked from drugs and alcohol.

Bourke, the dusty town, is filled with mischief and gossip and people just love to carry bad news about someone they know. His memories of the last time he was in Bourke were of a town that was set against him, and a town where the local cops bashed him, charged him and gaoled him.

He remembered being dragged from the courthouse in cuffs back to the watch house across the road. He remembered the stinking pissy smell of the cell they placed him in. 'Fuck Bourke,' he told himself, getting carried away in memories. And, he remembered the truck that transported him and four other black men later that same day away from Bourke and on to the Big House at Bathurst for another laggin.

Blackie was having difficulty in staying focused and was abruptly brought back into consciousness from Rips asking him 'if he was right?'

'Course I'm right, Rips ... Whatcha fucken talkin bout?' Blackie joked.

Blackie's lighthearted reply had everybody at the table less tense than they had been the minute before.

The young woman began again telling Blackie that 'dey all still talkin bout you back 'ome'.

'Fuck 'em!' he replied, shrugging his shoulders and shutting down the topic.

The woman acknowledged that he would not be drawn into a longer conversation about his identity or circumstances to her there at that moment by a nod of her head. As she lit a cigarette, Blackie asked, 'Who's your mob, sis?'

Chitchat followed, but Blackie could hardly hear above the noise in the bar anything that she told him. He smiled and took cues from her body language the best he could rather than repeating, 'What'd ya say?'

Back in Bourke, the talk was that Blackie was responsible for a firebomb attack on the cop shop, and that he had snuck out of town before the Riot Squad turned up. Rumours flew as cops belted black boys and black men they came across in a two-day splurge of unrelenting violence to teach the blacks another lesson of Who's the Boss. The same lesson the bastards have been trying to teach the blackfullas ever since they arrived here in Australia.

Blackie swore he wasn't there, that it wasn't him that threw the bottle.

But no one believed him.

He knew who did the deed, but was never gonna be a give-up on anyone he knew. He was thought of as being the type to carry out such a thing.

To the black folk, he was just another crazy nigga, and to the white people, he looked like he'd fit the bill in carrying out such an attack. The blackfullas might well have forgiven him for the attack on their mob by the police if he was there to take his punishment like the rest of the innocent when the time came for white payback. Because of all their lies and innuendos, he'd become a wanted man by the law, and an unwanted man amongst his own mob in the same moment.

Blackie noticed, and was satisfied, when Tegan ever so slightly lowered her eyes to indicate that she understood, and that she had been acknowledged as a country person from his mob. He was too wrecked to have a battle of wits with her at this point in time, to protest his innocence, so he left it at that. He straightened himself to an upright position at the table and casually reached for the fast-emptying pack of cigarettes.

With his head down, staring at the bubbles in his beer, nothing got past the keen eyes of Rips. He noticed the subtleties of what had transpired between Blackie and the woman that he was hoping to sleep with somewhere between then and morning, but he said nothing. The first chance he could get, he was gonna grab Tegan and scarper.

Carlos was interested in what Blackie and the woman were on about too. He raised an eyebrow towards Fingers to ask, 'What was that all about?' But Fingers had no idea why Blackie and the woman were in such a deep and meaningful convo. He shrugged his shoulders in an 'I don't know' gesture towards Carlos, leaving the matter unresolved for the Spaniard.

Carlos felt a tinge of jealousy towards Blackie. He wondered how it was that Blackie was able to have a special relationship with the woman while he wasn't even getting a look-in.

Staring at Blackie, Carlos spitefully asked himself, 'What the fuck have you got? Ya bastard!'

8

Fighting in the Dingy Bar

The crowded bar was becoming louder and hotter by the minute. Blackie felt his mouth dry from cigarettes and ran his tongue over his lips to relieve their dryness. Someone new was crooning the Hank Williams classic 'There's a Tear in My Beer' – badly – but good enough to get the crowd in on the act. Everyone at the table joined in the chorus together. Beer spilled everywhere as they sang and swayed. They sculled their beers like there was no tomorrow, and by the end of the song, the men's glasses were empty.

Blackie said, 'My shout! Gimme a hand, Fingers. Gimme a loan, Rips. Wait here bud till I git back. Jest in case ...'

Rips looked at Blackie and nodded. He knew Blackie had scores to settle, and might need backup if a fight started in the pub. Rips laughed hard and long and then told Blackie to ''urry up, cause there's a far, far, fucken drought on in the bush, and a man could die of thirst!'

The last time in Dubbo some local boys double-banked Blackie and gave him an awful flogging.

'Payback time tonight, boys,' he softly murmured, hoping to run into at least one of the dogs. 'Hey Rips, we might be sick, sad and sober in the morning, but we'll have a bit a fun tarnight,' Blackie warned.

Rips was feeling great, feeling Tegan, and having Blackie back on deck, cash in his pocket, music in the pub, and love in the air, ran his hand up higher on her thigh and smiled back.

'Fucken oath, brother, we will,' Rips answered.

Fingers and Carlos watched with interest all that coded work going on between Blackie and Rips, and between Rips and Tegan. But Rips had too many other pleasures on his mind to be bothered waiting around for Blackie and beer all night. As soon as Blackie was out of sight, he told Carlos to mind the table, that he had to go outside for a smoke and that he'd be back in a minute. No sooner he spoke than he was off with Tegan, outside and across the road into her car, loving her up all the way. He knew he was going to get lucky and delighted at the thought.

Nearing the bar, the speed was beginning to lose its effect on Blackie. He deftly felt his pocket, felt the satchel still there, smiled. He looked with a disconcerted eye towards the ever-swelling crowd filling the bar room. It was way overcrowded. He gently pushed his way through with Fingers sticking close behind.

'I gotta do a piss, mate. Wait here till I git back,' Blackie told Fingers.

Blackie disappeared into the men's room and had another slice of the speed inside the locked, pissy toilet cubicle.

After he had his swallow, he walked out from the bathroom and pushed through the sweaty sods and would-be entertainers, making his way towards the bar. Gassed up, he looked out to find Fingers. The moving crowd annoyed him and pushed up against him, making him feel angry. He pushed back, hard.

'Fucken people – move!' he yelled.

He began to struggle for air. He decided he'd grab Fingers and Rips and take them and their drinks outside for a line just as soon as he got back to the table. But, as he approached the bar again, he heard a voice raised in anger. He saw the crowd move in unison to make more room for what appeared to be a fight that was about to begin. As he broke through the crowd to see what was what, Blackie saw skinny Fingers being pushed and shoved around by a big, angry black man. Fingers was standing there, hopelessly outgunned by the bigger Koori man and being threatened by the black crowd as well; it appeared to Blackie that he was shaking in his boots.

'Whatcha fucken think you're doin 'ere, ya white prick?' the Koori yelled through pearl-white teeth.

Though he felt his heart weaken, Fingers stood his ground. He recognised the stand-over merchant as Tyrone Thompson, the Golden Gloves Champ – the local show-off. Tyrone, with the reputation as a cruel and dangerous brute. As good as he was with his dukes, he wouldn't let an opportunity pass by to rack up another cheap victory by flogging a drunken man who was too wasted from the booze. Nor would he let a chance slip by to stand over a man either too old or too small to make an equal fight of it. Fingers knew that if Tyrone threw a punch that landed, he'd be kissing the deck a second later. Tyrone towered over Fingers like a waterfall, feeling big.

Stuttering, words failed Fingers and it looked as though slaughter of the white man was on the cards for the entertainment of the bar. Fingers, sweating from fear, breathed a sigh of relief when he saw Blackie stick his head through the crowd. Tyrone clenched his right hand into a hard fist and was about to let fly when Blackie caught his arm and pulled him up. The crowd, eager to see blood, drew breath together and gasped in an expression of excitement as what appeared now to be a fight that would be worth watching, began to play out.

'What the fuck?' the bully exclaimed. 'Who the fuck are you?' he yelled.

Blackie pulled hard on Tyrone's arm and swung him halfway around to face him.

'Never mind who I am bud! What's goin on 'ere?' Blackie said, wildly.

'None-a-yar bizness!' Tyrone piped back.

Tyrone – surprised to see a man almost twice his age standing red-eyed, dirty and unshaven grabbing him – jerked his arm free from Blackie's grasp as he began to assess his chances.

Being just a little unsure of the situation he blurted, 'Who ya think ya are, man? You not from 'ere, so why don't ya fuck off?'

Blackie was in no mood to put up with the stand-over merchant before him. Blackie thought that the man loved himself, in the way Carlos admired himself, playing with his hair, grooming himself.

Having had enough of being told, Blackie teased, 'Where *you* from, brother?'

'Um from 'ere!' the bully replied, thumping his chest hard. He pumped himself up to his full height (all of six foot two), and looked down upon Blackie as he repeated himself, 'Um from 'ere! This is my country … and this is my pub!'

He thumped his chest hard again to show that he meant what he said, to show all that he was king of his own domain. Blackie knew the man's game and he'd become sick of listening to the fool. He felt the old familiar rush of blood as his legs began to shake and his heart thumped hard. He could hardly breathe. The only way he knew he'd stand a chance was to get the younger man outside where at least he'd be able to move freer.

Blackie had no idea who the young black man was, but he'd seen many bullies and tough guys who – mostly when push came to shove – were weak as piss.

'Your pub, ay? Well … you can shove your pub up

your arse! Better still, git out the back and I'll shove it up there for ya. Or ya too weak, "*brother*"?' Blackie challenged, hoping to shame the bully into it, outside.

Blackie wasn't waiting for a reply. He began unbuttoning his shirt as he pushed people sideways out of his way, making his way towards the back door. The crowd spread apart making room. The car park was muddy and big milky-coloured puddles lay cold and still upon the softened gravel ground. The crowd spilled out through the doorway and splashed all over the car park like spilt fizzy drink from a bottle. By the time the younger man walked out, a circle had been formed and in the middle of it stood Blackie, shirtless, and ready to rumble.

The younger man took his time to prepare himself. He ever-so-casually made Blackie wait until he removed his beautiful shirt, whilst a woman, his sister, claimed it and made herself useful as a coat hanger, further adding to his air of importance. The younger man was strong! Was fit. And Blackie was very quickly to learn that he could really fight. As they both swung into action, the younger man moved like a beautiful dancer. Well trained and confident in every move and gesture. Youth and good looks, on show. A black man involved in the dirty business of fighting another black man.

Blackie moved fast too. Wondered why it always seemed to come to this. He remembered really good boxers he'd trained with when he'd learnt the game. Different faces flashed through his mind. From the look of him, Blackie thought that the young man before him there was ready for a hard dig. He looked fit and powerful. But Blackie should have been paying more attention to the job at hand instead of thinking about other things.

Whack.

A punch caught Blackie. Blackie tasted blood. He wiped his mouth with the back of his hand and saw that it was covered in it. He felt dizzy. He felt sick. He needed time to get himself together again, so he played the oldest trick in the book: he stepped away from the younger man and, through bloodied lips, forced a smile. He then dropped his hands, and said:

'Good shot, mate!'

Tyrone wasn't expecting praise or acknowledgement from Blackie. Oh no, not at all. In fact, what he had expected was for Blackie to have bitten the dust, and to be laid out cold, like a bathroom tile. Tyrone's chest swelled with confidence.

But Tyrone had become a tad overconfident, and took more time out for all to acknowledge his power.

It was all the time Blackie needed to get his head back together and get back to business.

Blackie knew that he couldn't go punch for punch with the bigger man. He had to find some other way to stop him quickly. Tyrone moved towards Blackie, throwing punches so wild that they missed their mark. Blackie spoke silently to himself:

'Oops! Look out, blackfulla! Nuther one on its way ...

duck and move. Go southpaw, Black, see if he can handle that …'

'C'mon big-arse, where's all ya fight?' Blackie questioned.

Tyrone, enraged by Blackie's words, threw a big right cross that missed Blackie by a mile.

Blackie was in full swing at this point. He wasted little time in squaring up the fight.

Smash!

Blackie's left hook landed on Tyrone's jaw.

Up on his toes, Blackie mustered the strength left and said, 'Like that, ay? Try this, then!' Another punch hit Tyrone, hurting him more and confusing him at the same time.

Tyrone shook his head and made a savage snarl.

'If that's the best ya got, you're in a lota trouble, fuckwit!' Tyrone boasted.

Blackie followed the punch with a fast two-punch combo. His left rip caught Tyrone by surprise, landing hard in the soft pocket under his right arm. Tyrone winced, surprised at the speed and power that the blackfulla had. Attempting to cover his body from more shots, he dropped his right hand. That left him with his face wide open for serious damage. Too late he realised his mistake, and went crashing to the ground from the huge right-hand haymaker that Blackie had already let go.

Tyrone immediately sprang to his feet, full of energy and rage.

Through clenched teeth, he screeched, 'I'm gonna fucken kill you, ya black cunt! Then, I'm gonna fuck ya!'

Tyrone's blood was boiling and Blackie thought he meant every word he spoke. But Blackie knew too that he had the younger man in serious strife. Blackie prepared himself for the counterattack. He didn't have to wait long.

Tyrone rushed forward, swinging madly. A trickle of bright red blood seeping from the outside corner of his left eye caused the eye to close from the swelling. Tyrone threw haymaker after haymaker as he chased Blackie in hope that he might connect and down the bastard that was fighting.

He caught Blackie with a hard right hand. He was trying to land another big bomb on Blackie's head, to destroy him. To teach him just who was king. But in being too wild to be careful, most of his hard punches fell on Blackie's back and shoulders and caused no real damage. The weight of the whole affair, however, was beginning to tire Blackie. He felt his legs begin to tire and he gasped for breath.

Tyrone noticed the fatigue begin to take control of Blackie. This was the chance he was waiting for.

'You fucken cunt! I got ya now!' Tyrone swore. But Blackie moved just a little too fast for Tyrone to land the knockout hit. Tyrone grew wilder, throwing punches into thin air. The whole thing was wearing him out.

Blackie felt tired. He knew he didn't have much gas left in his tank.

He knew he wouldn't be able to take another bone-jarring, soul-destroying hit from the other man. His eyebrow was pissing blood that ran hot, down his face and into his mouth. He felt himself beginning to choke and he wanted to spew. He'd have to finish this quick, or he was dead for sure. He remembered his former boxing coach, old Keith, teaching him: 'Let 'em chase ya, son. Git outside and move fast. Hit 'im fucken ard! Take his 'ead off, and, then git outa there before he sees it!'

'C'mon and *fuck me* then, soft cock! Come on big-boy!' Blackie stirred.

All he thought he'd need was for Tyrone to make that one last mistake. So he teased and taunted Tyrone, to stay inside Tyrone's head and so he called to him again saying:

'C'mon! Here I am ... Fuck me!'

The teasing worked as Blackie hoped it could.

'Fucken kill you!' Tyrone screamed. He rushed blindly, head down, trying to tackle Blackie.

Blackie had him beaten and 'twas only a matter of seconds before it would be ended.

Blackie led Tyrone into a position where his face was completely unprotected. The opportunity that Blackie had been waiting for had arrived. Blackie let fly with a savage flurry of good punches that found their mark. The young man fell, crashing to the muddy ground.

The hard game of life left Blackie with little option other than to finish the fight, to get the business done and dusted. He didn't hate the young black brother he'd dropped, but he couldn't afford to let him up again either. Blackie's right hand felt as though it had a broken knuckle, and in any case, he knew it was useless as a weapon for he could no longer make a fist out of it. The only thing he could think of to do was to iron the other man out and get this over and done with once and for all.

Blackie's right boot landed straight on the man's mouth … the 'sleeping sickness' arrived on time with its devastating effect, sending Tyrone into instant unconsciousness.

Laying in the mud, all splattered, Tyrone presented a sad and pathetic picture. Just for a moment, Blackie stood there in silence, looking at the foul, terrible thing he had done.

The hometown crowd stood shocked and silenced. Blackie thought that the last thing on their minds was to see Big Tyrone destroyed and fucked up in the mud.

A sobbing woman ran forward, screaming, 'Isn't there a fucken man 'mongst youse? Look at my brother!' she cried, pointing at Tyrone.

'You mongrel black cunt!' she screamed at Blackie.

The crying woman tried to rouse her brother. She held Tyrone's head in her arms. She sobbed for him, shaking him, trying to bring him around. But his head flopped from side to side. He bled all over her arms and dress. Her insults stirred the crowd into a collective action. From every direction they rushed Blackie to exact some revenge on behalf of their wounded warrior.

Blackie was too tired to fight anymore and he knew he was done for. As soon as the first punch from the maddened crowd found its mark on him, it splattered him. The mob attacked savagely, without sympathy. Their intention was to cause as much damage as possible as they proceeded to kick the shit out of him. They fell over themselves in their rush to get in the action. They each wanted to take home their own 'special' story of how they smashed Blackie to bits. They would then feed off their made-up and extravagant yarns for weeks after. Exhausted, brave, but beaten, Blackie collapsed in a heap as punches and boots rained from above. He did his best to cover his face and groin as he tried to curl tightly into a foetal position. But it was impossible to protect or to defend himself in that moment. There were just too many. So Blackie took the medicine. Splat! Kick! Oh!

At one point during the beating, he knew there was something dreadfully wrong; he felt a sharp burning pain in his side.

'Fuck!' he cried.

Heavy boots found their mark on him. They knocked Blackie out in the rush and though he was out cold, still the crowd kicked him, their sense of pleasure being fuelled with every blow they'd land. It was only the distant sound of rushing cop sirens that saved Blackie in the car park. The police cars sped with their lights flashing through the mid-western night.

Gathering Tyrone up, the mob scattered quickly. The motionless body of Blackie lay blood-soaked and still, in the emptied car park. Fingers rushed in and tried to carry Blackie away. But Blackie was too heavy for Fingers to carry by himself. Fingers kept slipping in the mud and, just when it looked hopeless, Silvia, the woman Blackie and the boys had helped out at the cemetery (who had been buying cigarettes at the drive-through), saw Fingers, and rushed to help. Together, they managed to drag Blackie off into the dark and away to safety just as the first police car arrived on the scene.

9

Dot's Place

As Blackie came round, he softly whispered, 'Jasmine? Nan?'

Jasmine was his grandmother's favourite perfume: she must be near, he thought. He tried to get up from the small bed he found himself on, but was held back by soft but firm hands. He was too weak. His eyes slowly adjusted to the light.

He found himself shirtless on a single bed in a darkened bedroom.

'What?' he asked himself.

Coming into focus, he was relieved when he recognised Dot attending to him. She had that look about her that she had when she was full of business. She washed blood and muck from his face, paying particular attention to a deep gash that continued to bleed at the corner of his eyebrow. Dot flashed a small torch into firstly one eye, and then into the other. Blackie could see her mouth opening and closing, but he couldn't hear her voice.

Blackie felt pain everywhere from the bashing. Slowly, he began to remember what happened. Images of boots and mud flashed across his mind. He'd been beaten by better men, but he couldn't remember when. He looked at Dot and tried to smile.

She looked at Blackie and said, 'G'day, cuz. Where ya bin?'

Blackie cracked a smile through cracked lips, happy that his hearing had returned, and quietly said, 'I come back from the city. I bin livin on the wire. I love ya, me old cuz,' he said, closing his eyes and falling asleep again.

Being as tough as the boys when growing up, it generally took a lot to make Dot cry or show outright emotion. But she always had a soft spot for Blackie. Big tears left stain marks on her dry cheeks. Blackie and Dot were the best of friends, as well as being first cousins. Dot made accommodation for him from the time they hit kindergarten together. She took his part and dropped bigger kids who tried to intimidate him at school and she stood up to those who would try the same game on the street. Dot didn't win every fight, but she let all know that she was game, and, that alone gave her a fearsome reputation. Watching Dot going punch for punch with boys and girls, standing up to teachers and adults who would threaten and bully her, was good training for Blackie in learning to use his fists, and to stand his ground.

'Git away, Blackie,' she said to him, trying to be strong for the both of them. 'Now, jest stay still there while I clean ya up,' she said to herself, trying to convince herself he'd be okay.

An hour had passed before he woke again. Dot was gathering bloodied towels and pieces of cloth into a laundry basket when she was surprised by Blackie.

'How bad is it?' he murmured. 'Am I gonna live?'

'Ya bloody ratbag!' Dot roused. 'Haven't you learnt anything yet? What ya doin goin gittin inter fights all the time for? Ya should be in hospital. You been knocked out. Need X-rays, boy! Bloody Fingers! Had no right bringin you here. Shoulda took you straight to hospital! Don't ya know you could die? Then where would we be, Black?'

'No hosp'l, sis, coppers. You know what they're like. Don't worry bout me, Dot. I won't die! Ancient 'Gyptians useda say, if ya call a man's name, he's not dead … So all ya gotta do is call me name, cuz. And I'll be there!' he joked.

Dot shook her head and thought about it for a while. She was puffed from all the work. Her fat body was getting too heavy for her to carry anymore, and her days of patching up drunken brothers and cousins were well past her best.

Dot softly closed the door on her way out, but not before she turned back and looked at him and then said, 'Yeah, but, you not Egyptian … you're Wiradjuri, ya silly bastard!'

Her words fell like ice into an empty glass.

Clunk!

Clunk!

Clunk!

Walking away, Dot knew the drill without being told the specifics.

Police would have been notified by the hospital staff as a matter of course when a patient in Blackie's state presented for treatment. She figured Blackie most likely would have been 'pinched' and held in the local lock-up until whatever charges they could find would have been laid on him. She knew the police hated Blackie, just as she knew that they despised most black men who refused to buckle under their bullshit. She had seen the damage they dished out to her father, and to her uncles and cousins. Cut eyebrows, torn ears, bleeding skulls, fractured knuckles and twisted knees, all injuries of race and race fights that Dot had been called on through the years to dress for her people. At all hours of the day and night bloodied and broken 'brothers' and 'sisters' dropped in for help from the compassionate one – Dot. She'd stitched her people back together and then the cops would tear them apart again. Coppers broke their bones in their effort to break the black man's spirit. She knew Blackie didn't know when to cry 'give' or when to walk away from the challenge. Blackie was born to lose the battle, and the war it seemed. Just the way it is sometimes. But that fact never stopped him from trying to get things right though, either. He'd written to ombudsmen and to newspapers. Complained about being 'verballed' and abused by different police officers. But nought came of it. So he gave up looking for help and justice from the system. It seemed that the cops were a law unto themselves.

THE COPS:
The best
Untouchables
money can buy,
– some say.

Dot did the best she could to put Blackie back together again. She was happy that most of his injuries appeared to be superficial; she worried though that there was internal damage. Her years of work in emergency rooms as a nurse was tested time and again by the various relations who'd turn up, busted up, beaten and broke all hours of the day or night looking for her to fix it all. Big Dot – a real angel to the blackfullas in Dubbo, she didn't ask for nothing in return for all she'd done for everyone who needed her help. There wasn't a Koori house in town that she was not welcome in. Such a shame to see her so sick. After the birth of her twins, she got diabetes. She had to quit the job at the hospital, and she did it tough, as Fingers had no work. Money was always tight, and kids and medicine cost a lot. Dot tried to lose weight, went on every diet she could find, but nothing worked. Some days she was as good as gold, other days the poor woman couldn't get out of bed.

Fingers gave her the full story – all except leaving out the bit about the woman that Rips returned to the table with, for fear of misunderstanding leading to a jealous row.

'That bastard, Tyrone from Wellington … He was pickin on me, and Blackie stepped in and took him on. They got into it behind the pub. Blackie dropped the bastard. But, that mob, ya know what they're like? They all got into Black. Silvia jest happened to be there gittin smokes at the drive-through and helped me drag Blackie away …' Fingers recalled.

Satisfied that Fingers could hardly do anything to prevent the fight, Dot rested whilst drinking a cup of sugarless black tea.

The night was a restless one, full of tormented images running wild through Blackie's mind. Pictures of caves and green fields, of buses and ambulances criss-crossing empty streets, of Christian crosses and men in blue uniforms and of men with no faces, kept drifting over and over in his mind.

The storm raged outside, and the wind howled a sorrowful noise. It shook the window panes and rattled the green doors of Dot's old house. And, as the dawn crept up on Dubbo with an unusually dark and gloomy presence, Nanny – Dot's kid's pet goat – snuggled in her home. Deep inside the old wrecked car in the backyard, Nanny kept herself out of the storm. Blackie lay still upon the single bed, watching shadows dance while counting flowers on the wall. Sometimes he imagined he could see faces of people he knew in the shadows that danced across the plasterboard. Other times, he thought the shadows were the shapes of bad spirits that had come to him to do payback for the dirty deeds he'd done dirt cheap.

'Huh. Huh. Huh. Brrrr,' he whispered.

He closed his eyes and reached to the floor for cigarettes. His fingers stretched as far as they could, left and right, and up and down, but neither packet nor single cigarette could he find.

'Fuck. Nuffin,' he said. He faded back to sleep.

Sore, from head to toe, he stirred to the wonderful sound of children's giggles. His head ached, and though still concussed, he was delighted and taken by surprise to find identical twin boys kneeling beside his bed. They were resting their heads between their hands, examining him closely. Blackie thought he was seeing double (as indeed he was), though, and rubbed his eyes to make sure he wasn't. He gently reached out, and, with trembling fingers, touched the boys' faces.

'Now! Who are you two little Murris, hey?' he asked.

He rolled onto his side and rested his head on his arm in order to get a better look at the lads. The youngsters smiled, just like kids do when they discover something different; their eyes shone like diamonds.

'Who you?' asked one boy.

'Whatcha doing our place?' asked the other.

Blackie smiled back at them.

'Um ya uncle Blackie, thas who I is. Now, who are you?' Blackie said.

'I'm Vincent! Bet ya can call me Vince, if ya like,' answered the first lad.

'And I'm Ralph. Bet you can call me, Rrrrralllph!' said the other.

Both boys fell about themselves laughing.

'Well, that's very generous of ya. Vince and … Rrrrralllph!' Blackie joked back.

'How come you is our uncle? Where you come from?' Vincent asked politely.

'Because, well … I jest am, thas why! Um your mum's cousin. But I've been living down in Sydney for a long time, thas how come you two don't know me. Hey, how old are you fullas?' Blackie asked.

'We are six!' said Ralph, showing off.

'Nup. Not yet we ain't! Not till six a'lock Mum said, Ralph!' corrected the observant Vince.

Vince said it and pushed his brother sideways, knocking him off his bended knees onto the floor. No harm done. Ralph sprang back up, and a game of push and shove started and ended in good fun with neither boy none the worse for the experience.

When they finished Ralph said, 'Yeah, well we nearly six, then!' He poked his tongue out to Vincent, who did the same back.

Blackie watched in wonder the fun and love the brothers shared with each other. He thought of the fun times he had had with McWilliams when they were young, before things went bad and McWilliams turned into a dog who lied and dobbed Blackie into trouble.

'What happened you?' little Ralph asked, after the shoving had come to an end quietly.

Blackie saw the fear in the boy's eyes. He assured them that he was alright, that he just had a bit of an accident that was all. Blackie didn't like lying to children; however, he didn't want to give them another chance to ask further questions about his bruises. He quickly changed the subject saying,

'Ahh. So youse are big birthday boys, hey? Not little baby boys, ay? Well, are ya gonna have a birthday party or what?'

'Yeah. Tanight!' both boys answered in unison.

Their little faces beamed with glee in the knowledge that today was their special day.

'Ya reckon ya can invite ya old uncle Blackie then?' Blackie asked, trying to sound excited if he was allowed to attend.

Both boys looked at each other, and then back at Blackie, and then back at each other again, before they nodded their heads in agreement that it would be alright if he came to their celebration, that he could have some cake. The boys returned to their original position with their head between their hands as they closely examined Blackie once more. Blackie liked the boys from the moment he opened his eyes and found them there. There was a mischievous twinkle in their eyes that expressed innocence.

The moment was broken when the voice of the twins' mother called for them to 'Git away, and stop disturbing Uncle Blackie!'

The boys said a quiet 'see ya later', and left, hurrying back to their bedroom, both pushing each other to see who could be out the door first.

Blackie lay there for a while, and then struggled, as he slowly sat up. He needed to piss. He groaned and moaned in pain and regretted getting into another fight that resolved nothing, and only served to remind him that he was no teenager with teenage strength and springiness.

'Fucken stupid cunt!' he cursed himself.

He cursed himself all the way as he awkwardly made it through the bedroom doorway and down the hallway into the bathroom. Thankfully for him, the bathroom was right next to the room he'd been sleeping in, so he didn't have far to stagger, and thankfully too, he had the wall to cling to for support all the way there. And he cursed himself all the way to the toilet, wishing he hadn't had another stupid bloody fight. He entered the spotlessly clean bathroom that smelt of lavender. He steadied himself against the wall as he pissed into the white toilet bowl. The clear toilet water turned red from blood in his piss. He knew from past experience that his damaged kidney was bleeding again. His kidney was first torn when he was sixteen years old playing football. A big blockhead forward dropped a knee into Blackie's back and ruptured the organ. Ambulance officers whisked Blackie to hospital and he was warned to never play again, that his kidney would always be subject to damage should he be hit in that region again.

He was told not to exert himself by the specialist in Sydney, but he only seemed to remember the warning when it was all too late. The sight of red urine made him stand up a bit straighter and take notice. The reality of internal damage came into clear view in the cold, hard light of the day.

'Not a-fucken-gain!' he swore.

He looked at it, and then he flushed it away. Worried, he turned and washed his face. He slowly dried himself, and then studied his face in the mirror. Both eyes were the colour of slate, and the big cut near his eye (that had been cleaned and dressed by Dot), swollen and closed with congealed blood. 'Still got one good eye,' he whispered to his reflection.

'Shit!' he said.

He looked as bad as he felt – deathly grey, and black and blue.

He felt like throwing up. He made it back to the toilet just in time as he began to vomit. After a couple of goes of dry retching, he threw his guts up – mostly beer and bile shot from his stomach and that burnt his throat on the way out.

*

Dot could hear him from her bedroom, but she said nothing. She sat there listening. She felt sorry for him, but also knew that he'd either get tough or die from the way he was living. It seemed that no one, or nothing, could settle him down to live a quiet and peaceful life. Dot wondered what Blackie was doing in Dubbo.

'He say anything to you last night?' she asked Fingers.

'Bout what?' Fingers answered.

'Why he's here?' Dot continued.

Fingers thought about it for a while and said, 'Naa. Jest picked me up in Lonely Street when I was going to the paper shop, and then we went to the pub.'

Dot leant back on the cushions and looked around the place. She was searching for the true answer to her question. Her bedroom was filled with photos and things, with gifts – unopened beneath her bed, with slippers and shoes and with Fingers' cowboy books and comics. Her eyes came to gaze upon a photo of her and Blackie, looking shiny in school uniform, in a class photo from 1980 when they were young primary-aged kids. She reached and took hold of the photo and examined it closely. 'Look at us then.' She spoke, showing Fingers the picture. Looking intensely at the photo, Dot spotted a boy standing behind Blackie in there.

'It was him – Blackie! He did it, I saw him!'

Dot could still hear McWilliams' scared voice telling other kids when the library burnt down. Blackie, now in his late thirties, never forgave him, and Blackie never forgot the sting of accusation from the white boy who was once his friend.

'Friend! Huh! Bullshit. More like brothers, them two,' Dot said. 'They did everything together before McWilliams lied about Blackie.'

It was *then* she understood why Blackie had returned.

The big bush outside her window banged hard on the pane. Thinking of bad omens, the banging bush shook Dot up a little. Dot and Fingers heard Blackie flush the toilet again, and heard him shuffle away, cursing himself all the way back to the bedroom. Figuring that she knew why Blackie was back in town had brought about a change in Dot's face. She looked worried and scared about what she thought Blackie would do that could bring harm to her and the family.

Fingers asked, 'What? What's wrong?'

'I know why he's here. Wait here, I wanna talk to him!' she said.

She left Fingers alone in the dark bedroom and went in to see Blackie.

Blackie was sitting on the side of his bed, feet tapping the floor. Dot sat beside him, and looked at the floor. A long minute passed when she turned to Blackie and said, 'I know why you're here, cuz.'

Blackie turned to look at her. He studied her face and saw in her eyes that she was telling him the truth, that she had worked him out. He nodded and looked down at the floor.

'You can't stay here, Blackie. Not if you're here to do

that! I got kids, I can't have police runnin through the place with guns and stuff, not no more,' Dot told him.

'Thas alright, cuz. I'll go out ta Mum. Been wantin to go out to the old Mission for a long time now, anyway,' Blackie replied.

Dot hated what she had to say next even more than telling him that he couldn't stay at her place. But, if he was going to bring the police force into her home, then she wouldn't stand for that violence around herself or her family. She sucked in a deep breath.

Blackie heard the fear in her breath. He looked to see her eyes filling with tears. He put his arm around her and she leant, crying on his shoulder.

'It's alright, cuz. I won't bring the coppers here,' he said, trying to reassure her.

'It's not jest that, Black,' Dot said, drying her face. 'That's Radjuri Land Council ground now. Ya gotta be a member ta git on there,' she continued.

Blackie thought for a while. His blood was getting hot. Membership to get on the country of his birth ... The same land that he once had access to freely, had now become private property, owned by a local Aboriginal land council and requiring membership for anyone to be there.

'They can't do that, the bastards!' he growled. 'My mother's buried there! They can't stop me ...?'

They both knew that Blackie had no place in Dubbo to hide, and that there was too much danger for all if he hung around and went to war with the cops. They looked at each other with sad eyes.

'She'll be right,' he said, 'I'll git goin soon as I'm better. Don't worry, I won't bring 'em here,' he promised.

Dot left him on his bed and went to see what the kids were up to.

Blackie sat wondering where Rips and Carlos had gotten to. He had to find a way out of Dubbo, and wanted them to help. He hoped that Rips behaved himself and brought no harm or danger to Tegan last night, with his demand for sex or whatever he wanted from her. He tried to focus on the wind and on the rain that was lashing the house. For some unrelated reason, he started reciting Coleridge's classic poem 'The Rime of the Ancient Mariner' silently to himself.

Water, water, everywhere,
And all the boards did shrink;
Water, water, everywhere,
Nor any drop to drink.

After that, he thought of the Gordon Lightfoot song, 'The Wreck of the Edmund Fitzgerald'.

With the morning there was no let-up from the wild weather. The storm outside turned more savage, more outrageous. Garbage bins were being tossed in the air like paper. The wind that had chopped through the night was now chopping through the dawn. It was doing its best to tear Dubbo apart at its seams. The storm might well have been strong enough to sink the old Fitz. Blackie's mind raced from one thought to another –

a by-product of the hangover from all the speed he'd taken the day and night before in the toilet at the pub. He'd told Dot that he was too crook to eat, and that the only thing he needed was a drink of water and to rest up a while until his head stopped spinning. As if things weren't bad enough for him,

He was coming

Down, Down, Down.

His hands shook like that of an old man with the tremors.

Lost in thought, he thought he could hear voices. He hummed a tune from 1962, and thought it funny for no particular reason. He thought about things that made him laugh. Silly sayings like when people speak saying, 'No. Yeah, blar, blar, blar ...' He looked into the darker parts of the room – behind the door, between the gap of the bed and the wall, but he couldn't see anyone lurking there. The voices he imagined he could hear remained just out of range for him to make out what they were saying. It frustrated him. He had lied when he said he was alright, and that once he had another sleep, he'd be right as rain.

10

Boys' Talk

In the other room, Fingers heard a car door slam. He cautiously pulled back the blind to check who had come to the house. 'Rips!' Fingers spoke. He saw Rips dressed in brand new clothes, arm in arm with Tegan, walk towards the front door.

'Um, lookin for Blackie,' Rips stammered as Fingers opened the door. 'Someone said you brought 'im 'ome 'ere last night, ay? He alright?' he continued.

'Yeah,' Fingers said. 'He's layin down in the back room there.'

Tegan, a cousin of Dot's, disappeared into the lounge room as the men headed towards Blackie's room. Fingers led Rips up the narrow hallway, to the little room at the end of the house. Halfway along the hall, Fingers propped and turned back to face Rips.

'Come here, mate,' Fingers said as he led Rips into the children's bedroom.

'Whas a matter?' Rips said, surprised.

It took Fingers a second to find the right words to say. Finally he asked, 'Do ya know that this fella talks to himself?' Fingers pointed a thumb towards the room Blackie was in.

Rips smiled and softly said, 'Yeah, the silly bastard been doin it for years. Reckons it helps 'im sort things out in his mind when 'ees 'sleep, or some shit like that. Don't worry bout it, man. He's okay,' Rips assured Fingers.

Fingers seemed a little relieved, and then together, they made their way towards the end bedroom where Blackie was sleeping. As they approached the door, they could hear the unmistakeable soft mumbling of Blackie's voice. Without knocking, Fingers gently opened the door. Blackie was dozing on the single bed, covered only by a cotton sheet. He was smiling and whispering to an invisible entity.

'How much did ya say that was, brother?'

Fingers and Rips looked at each other. When Fingers met Rips' eyes he found it hard to stop himself laughing out loud. The bedroom floor was littered with dirty tissues and a bloody towel, all evidence of Blackie's suffering. His lips were swollen and cut. His eyes, puffed and purple, looked as sore as they were swollen. A big bruise coloured both eyelids. Dried blood still clung around his mouth, all evidence of Blackie's pain. Rips' joy quickly turned to outright rage and shock to find Blackie in such a busted-up shape.

'Fuck-me-dead, Blackie! Who did all dat to ya?' he blurted out.

Blackie stirred. Looked up through his one good eye to find Rips standing, worried, beside him. Blackie tried to smile, but found the best he could do was to pull a sad old grin. He coughed to clear his throat and tried to reach for the water bottle beside the bed. Rips hurried to help and retrieved the bottle for him.

'Fuck, Blackie! Who did all that to ya, man?' Rips demanded in an angry voice.

Blackie saw the anger in Rips' look, and he hastened to assure Rips that it was no big deal.

'No b, b, b, big deal, be fucked, Black! Who did it? Ya right? Or what?' Rips said, getting wilder by the second.

Rips' top lip curled, as was always the case when he was stirred up. Seeing Blackie in a busted-up state made Rips' blood boil, and if the culprit or culprits responsible for Blackie's demise would have been in spitting distance from him, he woulda let 'em have it. Fingers, sensing that he might somehow end up being blamed for Blackie's injuries, decided to make a quick exit and leave the two black men alone to talk business.

'I'll put a cuppa on, hey?' Fingers asked, but didn't wait for a reply.

After Fingers left, Blackie said to Rips, 'Never mind, brother. Sit down 'ere, I wanna talk to ya.'

He patted the bed, and Rips accepted the offer and sat at the foot of the bed. After taking a swig from the water bottle, Blackie offered it to Rips who replaced it beside the bed.

'Ay! Where'd ya git the new clothes from, bud?' Blackie inquired upon noticing the new attire Rips had set himself up in.

'Ya won't fucken believe it, Black!' Rips exclaimed, sounding like an overexcited kid who had thought all his Christmases had come at once. His big face beamed as bright as headlights and his smile was big like that of a rodeo clown, 'I won the fucken big link up, man! Ten grand! On da pokies, bra!'

He couldn't contain his excitement and grabbed Blackie's arm hard to convince him that he was telling the truth. Blackie buckled a bit under his grasp. Rips released his grip and moved slightly away. Blackie settled comfortably against the wall. He propped himself on one arm. He looked at Rips, dressed in fine new jeans and shirt.

'Pocket full of gold hey? Fuck you're arsey, big fulla!' Blackie congratulated him. 'Whatcha gonna do with all that cash, ay?'

Blackie got Rips to open the window, and then put the bite on for a cigarette. The first long drag made his head spin so bad he thought he'd blackout. He rested against the wall until his head cleared listening to Rips' plans regarding his newfound wealth.

'Well, I haven't got it all yet! The bastards down there only gib me a thousand last night, man. Git da rest today,' Rips boasted. 'Um gonna git a car and go 'ome and see me old mum. Heard she's in 'ospital back in Walgett ... Suppose I'll give her most of it,' he finished.

Blackie smiled and said, 'Thas good, bud. Ya better off givin it to your mother. You'll only end up drinkin yaself to death anyway!'

Blackie wanted Rips to stay. Wanted to go back to the big smoke with him. He tried to convince Rips by saying, 'Bet listen, mate, don't go home. Jest put the money in ya mother's account, man. Something bad's gonna 'appen, Rips. I got a bad feelin brother.'

'Whatcha fucken talkin bout, Blackie? I been 'ome thousand times. Um too smart for them cops up there. I'll be in and out 'fore they even know I was there!' Rips big-noted himself.

'Naa bud. I got a real bad feelin bout this one, Rips! Stay 'ere, mate. I'll be up and round again in a couple-a days.'

'Don't go talkin like that, Blackie. Yul bring me bad luck, man. This the best thing ever 'appen to me, man. I'll be able ta give Mum somefin back for all the stuff I put her through ova the years. Don't say stuff like that, man,' Rips whinged.

He was worried about Blackie's request. He knew better than to doubt him about most things like this. He wanted to go home so bad, to show all of his mob how well off he was, to big-note that he finally had something most of them could only dream about. He was rich! He had been secretly summing up presents he'd give to particular relatives and imagined the smiles and looks of astonishment on the faces as he played the black Santa Claus – maybe a new bike for his nephew, Kevin ... Gift vouchers for his nieces ... Chocolates for his aunts ... Grog for his uncles.

Rips felt uncomfortable and regretted now that he'd

come to check on Blackie in the first place. Unable to take it anymore, Rips smiled, shook his head and said jokingly, 'You a silly bastard Blackie when ya wanna be. Ya wanna look after *yaself*! Look at ya! I thought ya could fucken fight! Ya look like ya had the shit kicked outa ya!'

Blackie sat up a bit straighter and said sadly, 'I had the shit kicked outa me!'

Rips was only joking, and thought he'd hurt Blackie with his sarcasm. He hastened to repair things by saying, 'Fair dinkum, ay? Wait'll I git back, brother. We'll see how good these Dubbo dicks are then. I'll only be gorn couple-a days.'

He lit two cigarettes and handed one to Blackie. Rips then reached deep into his trousers pocket and pulled out a fistful of dollars. He shoved the lot into Blackie's other hand.

''Ere. Buy yaself some smokes or somefin while um gorn,' he said.

'Fuck man! How much is all dis? I don't need all that, brother. I git paid tomorrow. 'Sides, these fullas here are lookin after me. You keep it, mate.' Blackie tried to give the money back, but Rips would hear none of it.

'Ya give me plenty, Blackie. Ya might wanna score while um gone. You keep it,' was the final word said on the subject as Fingers came through the doorway holding a small tray with three cups of steaming tea.

Fingers was about to set the tray down when an enormous thunderclap shook the house. He almost dropped the tray into Rips' lap. Blackie laughed to see Rips move so fast. Then both black men stared solemnly at each other as they read the thunderclap as a sign – a bad omen.

'Fuck ya, Blackie! Ya got me jumpy now, too!' Rips laughed.

'See man! Told ya. Signs all over the place!' Blackie laughed back.

Rips was shaken and visibly frightened by the words, and the thunder that seemed to come on demand, emphasising Blackie's words. Rips obviously thought that the Blackman could tap into some other world – into the world of ghosts and spooky things.

'Far, far, faaark ya, Blackie! Ya wanna stop livin with ghosts! Ya got me shaky, man!'

Blackie winked at him, smiled and said nothing.

'A man's gotta do what a man's gotta do, I suppose,' Blackie softly considered to himself.

He decided to change the subject and asked Fingers what he thought Rips should do with his newfound fortune. The men sat and sipped their tea thoughtfully. Fingers said he had a mate that understood stocks and bonds and offered to put him in touch with Rips if Rips wanted to play the stock market.

'Fuck that, mate,' Rips said. 'I'm lucky to be playin with meself these days. 'Sides, they rob ya, dem 'countants and banker fullas, hey Black?'

Both men had seen their fair share of white-collar crims come through the system over the years to be wary about anyone holding their money for them.

'Only safe place for ya cash, in ya own sky rocket!' Rips declared.

'Does funny things to people – money, hey?' Blackie said thoughtfully.

Tiredness, once more, beckoned him to sleep. Its cool, dark hands crept into his brain. Blackie felt the hands stroke his eyes shut. He drew a deep breath that seemed to hurt the rib and cartilage in his chest. He let out a soft, slow groan that went unnoticed by the others.

'Naa. I reckon people are jest strange. Money's jest an excuse for people to be arseholes to each other,' Fingers said.

'The concept of wealth is a very particular thing,' Blackie lectured.

Both Rips and Fingers agreed with a nod of their head.

'People look at people different when they're rich. And, I think you're right Fingers. People can just be arseholes anyway,' Blackie finished.

The talk dried up and the long minutes drove each man back into his own private thoughts.

They all heard the rain falling heavily and it looked like it would for a while longer too. The midmorning sky was a complete grey, as grey as grey could be. The wind gusted and small trees planted along the side fence bent and struggled to hang on. The house shook with each gust. Blackie didn't like the sound the wind made as it tore at the world.

'Bad news wind, that fulla,' he said softly – way too soft for Rips and Fingers to hear.

Leaning against the wall, he remembered the junkies leaning outside the chemist, back in Katoomba. Yesterday, a lifetime ago to him. The memory of the broken eggs on the road came to his mind, making him feel sorry for himself, being busted and broken. He turned his thinking to the cemetery. He thought of the cold air around Nan's grave. He smelt the air, hoping to smell her jasmine scent again.

Suddenly Rips cooeed in joy. 'Ya fucken beau-tey!' he screeched excitedly. 'Won't be any cops on the road tanight if this rain keeps up. I'll 'ave a free ticket all the way 'ome. See, it's all fallin into place for me! You watch and see if um right or not.'

Blackie shook his head. Disappointed. 'It's not your gittin there, brother, it's the gittin out I'm worried about for ya. It's like Hotel California … even when ya check out, ya never leave!'

'You'll be right, Blackie!' Rips said to close down the conversation on the matter once and for all.

Blackie took the hint and shut up.

'Where's that little one from last night, man?' Blackie asked – referring to Tegan.

'Don't 'ave ta worry bout her Black. I, I, I lub 'er. She's the best thing that's 'appened to me in a long time. Sh, sh, she's coming with me when I go 'ome,' Rips said.

Blackie looked hard at Rips and could see that the man meant what he said. Blackie was taken aback by the unashamed honesty in Rips' tone and demeanour.

Blackie thought a love born in a storm such as this one they were all caught up in would be either deadly-strong, or doomed to fail. No middle ground or room to move about in a game of pretend there. He didn't say that though to his mate, instead he made a joke of the seriousness of it all by saying,

'Far out, man! You look after her, bra. She's related to me,' Blackie warned. 'Hey Rips, you quick as dis big whitefulla 'ere when it comes ta women. Fingers fell in love jest like that first time he met Dot in Sydney, hey old mate?' Blackie said, snapping his fingers.

Fingers was the first to draw breath and reply with a laugh, 'Yeah ya bastard, Blackie! You went round tellin everyone that "Dot and the Blur" were at it in the back of that old car of hers, didn't ya!'

'Well, if you wanna go showin off ya white arse in the lane!' laughed Blackie.

The three enjoyed the moment. The relaxed mood allowed each the privilege to ask an intimate question of the others.

'Ya got a lot to say bout everyone else there, blackfulla. Where's your woman?' asked Fingers.

Blackie felt the smile slowly drain from his face. He fished for his wallet and drew from beneath cards and paper, a torn, tattered letter.

''Ere.' He handed the paper to Fingers to read. 'Thas why ... There – she's still the one! She's got me, bro – Yeah ... she's fucken got me!' he said.

'Who the fuck *are* you?' Fingers asked him, reading the letter.

... I dunno what to say Blackie. I can't get enough of you. I want to go again and again. Your voice is like the whisper of the trees, and I want to be in the big world with you, looking into the Milky Way. I want your hands pulling me onto you. And your voice! Your voice is my embrace. But I won't wait for you to come back this time. This time, it's over for good. I love you ... but you know that.

xxx
Gillian.

The words seemed almost to tumble right off the page, and along the floor, under the doorframe and down the hallway, looking for any place to hide their shame. Blackie thought of her beautiful smile, those green eyes, her soft skin and those beautiful kisses. It had been nearly seven years now since he'd last laid with her. Sadly now, he remembered walking out on her one too many times.

'... it's over for good. I love you ... but you know that ...'

Fingers slowly raised his head and looked to see Blackie staring hard out the window. Blackie had found out the hard way that love is much more than a four-letter word. Blackie began to sing the Rolling Stones song 'Far Away Eyes'. Fingers held the letter softly and gazed again at the faded words on the dirty paper. He passed it to Rips who looked at it. But Rips couldn't read, so Fingers read it aloud before he passed it back to Blackie and joined Blackie in the chorus.

Blackie smiled a sorry smile of regret as he finished the song. '*She* had them eyes,' Blackie said, pointing to the letter, wondering what made such a sweet girl like her dance for a bastard like him.

The men fell quiet again. Fingers broke the silence with, 'Fuck, Blackie! Who wrote that letter, man?'

They watched Blackie collect himself and clear his throat before saying, 'Jest someone I used to know. The Force has been my boss for too long time now, boys. I've been sleepin under strange, strange skies, brothers. Fucked … I'm fucked.' And with those words, the time for talking about women had passed.

Fingers silently indicated to Rips to follow him out of the room.

He looked back at Blackie once more before closing the door softly behind them, leaving Blackie to recoup alone with his crooked dreams and desires. Fingers and Rips had another cup of tea and talked about the state Blackie was in.

'Fucken hell, Fingers … What 'appened to 'im?' Rips asked.

Fingers thought for a while then answered. 'He took my part with a Thompson from Wellington ...' Fingers began.

'Which one?' Rips interrupted.

'Tyrone ... Know him?' Fingers asked.

Rips rolled his eyes and nodded, yes.

'Well,' Fingers continued, 'he was looking to smash me because I'm the skinny whitefulla in the pub. Bet, Blackie stepped in and smashed *him* instead!'

'Yeah!' Rips said excitedly.

'Oh yeah. Blackie give it to him, alright. He can still fight, the cunt, hey? But afterwards, all the Wello crowd jumped him and tore him ta pieces ... Me and Silvia dragged him away jest before the coppers turned up. That's how come he's here, we brought him,' Fingers concluded.

Both men took the enormity of the situation in, quietly considering it all.

They wondered what was to become of Blackie. They agreed that the Blackman was headed for an early grave if he didn't take a pull and settle down somewhere quiet.

Rips found Fingers an easy man to speak with and so poured his heart out as a man is prone to do when full of speed and overjoyed with the possibilities of a new love in the offing. Rips reminisced about gaol times, and hard times he'd gone through, with and without Blackie, over the years.

'I membar dat riot at Cessnock – me and Black … Bout five years ago now … Dey put me and him in solitary for four days? Bashed the shit outa us, ay?' Rips recalled. He showed Fingers a half-inch scar above his eye from the batons used on him.

Fingers acknowledged and nodded, screwing his face up at the very thought of being smashed like that.

Rips spoke of his own mother, who was very sick in hospital, back home. 'Yeah bud, me ole mum, she's real crook, back 'ome in 'ospital. She's dying. Won't be long to go 'fore she goes. I gotta git 'ome ta see her.'

Fingers was a little saddened when Rips left, saying that 'he wouldn't be long', that he 'had to git smokes, and would be back'.

11

Dreamin at Dot's

Blackie woke in the midafternoon to the faint noise of people talking. He strained to hear who they were, but their voices were muffled by the storm that continued outside. Very gingerly, he made his way down the hallway towards the living room. He recognised Rips' laugh and the soft strumming of a guitar. Blackie was pleased to see him when he walked into the lounge room. The small crowd of Fingers and Dot, Vince and Ralph, Rips and Tegan, and a stranger woman and her baby presented a cosy picture. The mob gasped when they saw, bent before them, Blackie, with his face bloodied and bleeding again.

'Ya right there, bra?' Rips asked.

'Yeah, um sweet, man,' Blackie muttered.

He felt so seedy from drying out from beer and speed. He was as shaky as he was weak. Dot helped him back to the bathroom and patched him up again. Together they returned to the lounge room minutes later, Blackie looking a little fresher.

Silvia broke the tension with her bright voice, and

went and sat beside Blackie, asking, 'Hey. Remember me from last night, Blackie?'

Blackie looked at her, half-recognising her as the woman from the cemetery, and sat himself up a little straighter. He shook his head.

'Naa. Not really. Was you were at the cemetery?' he asked.

Fingers told him that it was Silvia (who had been buying cigarettes for her father from the bottle shop at the pub they were at last night) who had helped him drag Blackie away, and into her car, before the cops had shown up.

'Far out!' Blackie said. 'Youse know each other then, ay?' he asked.

The long and short of it all was that Silvia's mother was a close friend of Dot's. Dot had nursed Silvia's mum as she suffered with cancer. First Dot cared for the sick woman in hospital, and then, later, Dot nursed her at her home. During the end period, Dot had grown close to Silvia, and treated her as family.

'There ain't no secrets in this little country town, huh? Well, thas the good thing bout 'em, I s'pose. Everyone knows everyone. People help ya when ya in trouble. Thanks sis for gittin me away from there. But I don't remember much about it at all. Who was that bloke I had a crack at? He's got a big mouth, and a stand-over. Don't like bastards like that,' Blackie scoffed.

'Wello mob. You know him Black. He's a Thompson,' Fingers informed him.

Blackie nodded, thinking before he asked, 'He's a boxer, ain't he? Heard that name before. You know him, Rips?'

'Yeah, I know him. I know all his mob! I played footy against 'em in district games before. They all think they can fight a bit. Tyrone's Golden Gloves or somefin. Sta, sta, stand-overs and posers, thas all, the bastards. I downed big Leo – eldest bloke – years ago!' Rips said. 'Hit 'im in de guts and on da chin, and, Leo went arse-up.'

The boys laughed with Rips.

'You a fucken good'n'alright Rips, wished I was dere when you drove 'im,' Blackie said.

'Yeah, I got 'im alright, bruva. Two good hits – bang, bang! Big Leo was fucked in da dust!' Rips laughed.

Tyrone was reportedly a better fighter than his brothers. Silvia excused herself and disappeared into the kitchen where Dot was busying herself with cooking cakes and preparing food for the twins' party. The three men sat and chewed the fat and tried to pretend that the fight Blackie had got himself into the night before was over and done with by now, that there wouldn't be men on the street looking to finish him off if they ran into him.

Dot came back with a tray filled with cups, sugar and more boiling tea. Silvia followed her, carrying another tray loaded with cupcakes and biscuits. Everyone dug in, except Blackie. When Dot offered him some, he said, 'Naa. Not for me, Dot. Gotta watch me weight!'

They laughed and began to relax, and then Fingers

piped up and said, 'Hey, Dot? Whatcha think this means? I had a dream that I was in a plane, and it started to fall outa the sky. Everyone was screamin and stuff, but I just sat there. Everyone ran past me, staring at me. And, then the next minute, the plane jest landed safely and then I woke up!'

Dot, amongst her other fantastic abilities, was a renowned dream reader. She carefully considered the question, and then after some more pondering, replied, 'Well, you know how you feel like a fish out of water sometimes around my mob, when they jest talk over the top of ya and you're not recognised sometimes?'

'Yeah,' Fingers spluttered.

'Well, I think it's about that stuff. But this time, you're in the driver's seat, babe. You know deep down that people come to you when they're in trouble and stuff. I think the dream was someone talking to you, reminding you that you are a good man, and not to be frightened of anything,' she decided.

Everyone considered in silence what Dot had said before Blackie nodded his head in agreement and winked at Fingers saying, 'You da man alright there, big fulla!'

Silvia was the next to share her dream experience.

'I had a dream that I came into a lota money, and I got outa this rathole town!'

Everyone laughed. Rips stuck his hand up like he was a schoolkid or something and finished up by skiting, 'I, I, I deed! I deed! I deed won a lota money – last night! And I am gittin outa this rathole tanight!'

Discussion centred on how much was Rips' great fortune, and what he intended doing with his windfall. The conversation then drifted from one topic to the next with everyone putting their two bob's worth in along the way.

Fingers said that he wished that he had enough money to take Dot and the kids back to his country, back to New Zealand, to see the land of the long white cloud – to drink and eat from that country's great fortune.

'Long time since I've been home,' Fingers said sadly. 'It was beautiful in Auckland when I was young. Used to go to the bay with me uncles and fish all day. Plenty a fish there boys. Yeah. Beautiful.'

Dot said she wished that she could have her life all over again, just so she'd not make the mistakes she'd made along life's highway. Wished she'd never taken to drinking when she was a teenager. Wished that she'd spent more time saving money instead of spending it. 'Bet. I'm glad I met you my baby,' she said, looking at Fingers. 'You're a good man and worth more than gold to me …'

Fingers smiled his broken-mouth smile, turning red in the face.

'Love ya, Dot,' was all Fingers could utter, becoming choked.

Rips wished that he was as free as a bird, rich as a king, and to sing at the opera house to an audience of all his mates, with his mother in the front row, right next to Tegan! Tegan punched him on the arm and told him to stop being silly.

She said she wished she owned a big ship to sail to all the exotic places in the world.

Dot asked, 'What do you wish for, my cuz?' directing the question at Blackie.

Blackie thought about it for a while, and then said, 'Ahh, God. Nothin much. Place of me own, I s'pose.'

After a little while, the conversation was beginning to dry up.

'What do you dream about, Blackie?' Silvia asked.

Blackie glanced around, nervously, seeing the distance between them narrowing in each heartbeat. He got her intention right. Her question was as loaded as the Bible – full of promises of love.

It seemed she'd taken a shine to him, but he had a kind of indifference when questioned about love and affection.

He had his reasons – and they all related back to Gillian. He did never stay long enough in one place to make things work out with women.

Thinking of the woman who'd written the love letter he carried, and how she'd loved him, he spluttered, 'I don't dream, sister. Men like me. Don't dream.'

The words were hard for him to say, they felt like they were stuck halfway in his throat, but he somehow managed to cough them up. That put a dampener on everything. And Blackie regretted it. Oh no! He knew that he'd said too much, so he shifted away, towards the corner of the lounge, leaning on the arm rest.

He'd hoped that the harshness of his truth might turn

her off him. The moment caused all to stop speaking. They looked away from each other, waiting for something else to restart another conversation. A silent icy breeze snuck in under the door. The cold air made everyone shiver.

They looked at each other with wide eyes. All thinking about ghosts. The scent of jasmine came to Blackie's mind. His nan was calling him again. He still had business to finish with her. He felt the need to vomit and grabbed Rips' arm for assistance to the bathroom. They'd just made it to the bathroom doorway when he vomited. His spew flew into the tub, and onto the floor, as he staggered to the toilet bowl. The sour taste of his vomit burnt his tongue and gums.

'Gord! … Fuck!' he groaned.

Rips gently helped him to his feet as he reached for the washbasin. Rips turned back towards the doorway and saw the women with the young boys hiding behind their skirts, giving them the hint to leave. The spectators returned quietly to the lounge.

From behind, Fingers asked cautiously, 'Yar right dere, bruz?'

'Yeah, he be right. I got him,' Rips answered, without turning around. 'Shut the door there and I'll clean him up, bud,' he said.

Blackie washed his face, rinsed his mouth, squeezed a big blob of toothpaste on his finger, ran it back and forth over his teeth. The taste of the peppermint burnt the mouth ulcers more, but had the effect of leaving him with a cleansed palate. Exhausted, he collapsed back onto the toilet seat. Catching his breath, he looked at Rips, who just smiled and shook his head. From inside of a neatly folded handkerchief, Rips retrieved a small plastic satchel filled almost to the brim with fresh, base speed. Rips looked at Blackie and, without saying a word, offered the drug to him. Blackie looked up and, for a second or two, struggled with his ethical dilemma.

'Do I take the shit, or can I be strong and wait until the kids get their birthday party outa the way?' he asked himself.

But, the sour smell of the drug possessed a strong attraction. And, as usual, the speed had the best of him. So, with regret for his weakness (and in shame), he took the satchel into his shaky hand. He bowed his head as his guilt was plain to see, and then … the deed was done.

He found his little pocket knife and dug it deep into the speed. He withdrew the blade, full of the shit – way more than a gram. He licked the blade clean, screwing his face to the taste. He never hated himself more than he did right there. And so, he plunged the fucken knife back in again. And repeated the act. He wished he'd die from it. Then he remembered: 'Be careful what you wish for, blackfulla.'

He held the speed suspended in his mouth somehow without touching his ulcerated tongue for a few seconds, and then he rushed to the washbasin and gulped water from the tap to wash it all down. His mouth burnt, and his eyes watered more. As he stood bent over the basin, unsure whether he was going to throw up again or not, he passed the drug bag back to Rips. He passed the knife too, and then Rips dug in to get a big dose of the Force for himself. Blackie made way for Rips to drink from the tap by returning to the toilet seat. He buried his head into his hands and closed his eyes. He heard the tap being turned off, *creak*, and then Rips said,

'Ya right dere, cuz, or what?'

Blackie looked up feeling his heart beat wild in his chest and nodded that he was okay.

'Hey bruz,' Blackie said. 'How bout takin us down to the chemist?'

Without thinking about it, Rips said, 'Yeah. What ya wanna go down there for?'

'It's me guts. Look how swollen it is. Like I'm fucken pregnant or somethin. Git somethin ta make me shit or somethin. Haven't done a shit in about four days, or a week, I think. Maybe thas what's wrong with a bloke. And, me guts is real hard. It hurts, man,' Blackie moaned.

'You looked fucked alright, old mate,' Rips declared.

12

Ghosts in Black Skin

It was 4 pm. Tegan was driving them through empty streets towards the town centre. The gutters were filled with splashing water and Tegan's little car was being rocked as it rolled along. Blackie looked at the wild weather, loving its wildness. The Force had kicked him into life and he began to feel a bit better.

'Where we goin, man?' Blackie asked Rips.

Rips looked at Tegan, who seemed unsure of what to make of the strange question Blackie had come up with. He looked at Blackie to ascertain if the Blackman was pulling his leg or not. Seeing Blackie's glassy eyes shining like diamonds in a fog and the serious look on Blackie's face, Rips roared with laughter. Blackie was peakin. Rips felt the speed beginning to stir the good feelings inside his own head and was beginning to want Tegan again in the ways in which he had had her last night.

'Ya wanna go to da chemist, don't ya? Ya silly bastard!' Rips laughed.

'Huh? Ah, yeah, thas right. Fuck man, I'm wrecked!'

Blackie said meekly, before he too erupted into laughter.

The three enjoyed the stupidity of the moment. They laughed their way down towards Darling Street. Turning the corner, their joy quite abruptly turned to dread with the appearance of two police cars, speeding towards them with lights flashing, but speeding in silence without sirens blaring. They all held their breath and exhaled huge sighs of relief after the cops drove straight past them, without giving them a second glance.

'Yeah! Git fucked ya dogs,' Rips said aloud, watching the coppers disappear into the driving rain. 'Pity 'alp the poor bastard they're afta,' he said softer.

'Yeah – jest glad it's not us, bud,' Blackie answered nervously.

'Hey man! Where's the fuckwit?' Blackie asked.

Rips thought hard about the last time he'd seen Carlos.

'Hmm, thas right,' he replied. 'The last I saw him wuz at the pub last night. I told him to meet us back there this arvo. I'll go and have a look when we drop you off, ay?'

Blackie was glad to be inside the warm chemist shop. The rain made him hurry, and it made him cold. The chemist smelt clean like eucalyptus trees after rain. The smell took him back in his mind to times of his childhood – to times he'd went walking in heady heat before rain, to when all the birds fly, fly away, leaving the beautiful smell of eucalypt hanging all over the place. He remembered how he enjoyed following centipede tracks along the sandhills. He made his way slowly to the counter at the far end of the shop, only to be faced with a line of four elderly women. Three of them sat there, looking all bent out of shape in their motorised chairs, waiting patiently. The other woman stood resting on her walking frame while being served by a young white woman who looked splendid in her immaculate, white uniform. Blackie made his way to a chair and plonked himself on it. He closed his eyes and followed the action by listening to the conversations and the ringing of the cash register.

'Oh! Is that so?' the shop assistant over-emphasised, pretending to sound interested in the old woman's yarn about how bad they needed the rain. Blackie began humming softly the Creedence Clearwater Revival classic 'Bad Moon Rising'. The tone of the young woman bullshitting the old ones made him smile.

The warmth from the chemist heaters and the comfortable seat had Blackie relaxing, but the speed had him wriggling around in the chair. He forced himself to sit straight. He watched the last old woman being served.

When the business with the old woman was done the young woman returned to the cash register, and there she remained. Blackie made his way to the same place at the counter the older woman had just been served. He stood there expecting the woman to return and serve him. Instead, without turning to address him, she stared straight ahead, and asked in a snappy tone, 'Can I help you?'

'What's goin on 'ee-ya?' he asked himself.

He quickly came to the conclusion that he wasn't welcome in that shop, by that woman.

'Must be a "black" thing. Hmm? Wanna play games, ay, you little witch? Den, let the games begin!' he said to himself.

Blackie refused to answer the woman; instead, he stared away from her and gazed straight ahead, copying her pose. An uncomfortable few long moments elapsed before the woman repeated her question. This time, her voice betrayed her anger.

'Can I help you?' she uttered between clenched teeth. Still she refused to look at Blackie when addressing him.

And so, he stood there and refused to answer. 'See who outlasts who,' he told himself.

More uncomfortable moments passed until finally the woman stormed down to stand directly in front of the black man, with her small fists clenched tightly. She blinked and moved away a little in fear when she saw the busted face and the worn-out eyes of the Aboriginal man in front of her.

'Oh ... yes,' she gulped. 'How can I help you?'

But too late, by that time, Blackie was in a playful and vengeful mood. He decided that he'd have some fun with her before he'd let it go. Staring at her beautiful mouth and wondering how such spite could so easily spew forth from behind those soft, pink lips. He stood strong, secretly admiring her looks, and in a funny kind of way, admiring her willingness to not hide the fact she couldn't stand him.

'At least she's not too afraid to hide it.'

His eyes narrowed and he clenched his teeth, ahh, if only she'd been a man! He'd have bashed her there and then. He told himself that he would have exploded and used every ounce of the physical strength he possessed to crush and destroy the smugness. He would have cut loose to exact his revenge on the world in that split moment and cut her to pieces. But, he'd only have done that if she was a man!

'Are you deaf or something?' the woman snapped.

'Got ya!' Blackie said to himself, feeling happier that he'd made her react.

Blackie made out that he was straining to understand what she had asked him. He knew he could have just as easily been charming and polite as he could be the opposite when his anger kicked in. His gaze was very intent indeed as he made efforts to pretend to answer her by way of sign language. He touched each finger rapidly with the tips of the fingers from the other hand as he pretended to sign. He touched his mouth, his ear, his chin and then more rapid hand-fingering before he stopped completely and blinked pathetically as he stared at the woman for some kind of recognition and understanding. His hand signs were so fast that they looked like they could have come from someone who used hand signs as their first tool of language. It was good enough to fool her in any case. The woman stood transfixed and embarrassed by her behaviour.

She immediately drew herself together, however, and said, 'I'll go and get Doctor White for you.'

And without waiting for her customer to respond, she abruptly turned and walked away leaving Blackie staring at her tight arse as she left. He couldn't contain the broad smile that grew and spread across his face. For a short second, the joy he felt even overtook the pain from his gut. However his happiness, like all good things, didn't last long. He stood, bent at the counter, his stomach more swollen than before, and the pain was going from bad to worse. He was going to return to his seat when an elderly man wearing a bright, white lab coat suddenly fronted him with the pretty woman in tow, a few feet behind. The older man stood directly before Blackie and spoke slowly. He very carefully addressed Blackie, ensuring that Blackie had a clear view of his lips when he spoke.

'How-can-I-help-you?' he said slowly.

The old man expected that Blackie would be able to read his lips. Seeing the effort the old bloke was going to in order to serve him, found Blackie feeling shame.

'Ahh! Ya never thought this one through, did ya?' Blackie cursed.

His eyes looked down to the floor, to show the old bloke respect.

Blackie then said, 'Look mate. I'm crook. I need some painkillers.'

Hearing Blackie speak surprised and puzzled the old man. The young woman's head peered from behind the old man, and if looks could kill, Blackie would have been a dead duck right there, right then. Her dark eyes directed their disdain and hatred deep at Blackie. She didn't have to say a word. Her mouse-face said all that she wanted to, to the black man who had just made a fool out of her in front of her boss.

Blackie raised his head slowly, and drew himself up as straight as his twisted stomach would allow to challenge the fierce stare that the woman was directing at him. Blackie's return stare at the woman commanded attention. Blackie held the floor. Neither the old man nor the young woman had any idea what he was playing at.

Although his face was bruised and he was bunged up around the eyes, his eyes shone bright. Thanks partly to the speed he'd taken, he gave the impression that he was completely in control and in charge of the situation that they found themselves tied up in. He frightened the woman and the old man.

'Whatcha see when ya look at me?' Blackie said softly to the woman.

The softness of his voice, coupled with embarrassment that he'd caused her, turned her angrier, and filled her with rage.

'Nuffin!' she spat.

Her eyes narrowed just so slightly with her anger and, without speaking again, she spun on the spot and stomped off into the back of the shop out of sight.

'Yeah. That'd be fucken right,' Blackie swore.

The old man didn't know what to make of it all. He

obviously felt threatened by Blackie's behaviour and by Blackie's presence. He repeated his original question to Blackie.

'How can I help you?'

'Mate, I need some painkillers, and, something to make me go to the toilet. Me stomach's real sore,' Blackie said shyly.

The old man's experience and training told him that Blackie's injuries could very well be serious enough to cause him major drama.

'What happened to you?' asked the old man.

'Was workin on the silo. Out Dunedoo. Fell off scaffold,' Blackie lied.

Blackie was thinking on his feet as quickly as he could. He didn't want too many questions. He could feel his shirt begin to stick to his sweaty skin. He wiped his forehead with the back of his hand and felt the clamminess from his brow stick to his hand. He just wanted to get some laxatives, and perhaps some Panamax (or something stronger), and to get out of there.

'Listen, young man. Your injuries could be life-threatening. You need to get yourself to the hospital immediately,' the old man warned.

Blackie did his best to convince the old man that he was alright, and that if he could get his laxatives and pain relief, he'd be on his way. However, no matter how Blackie put it, the old man wouldn't give in to the mad request.

'You really shouldn't have anything before you see a doctor, my friend. I could be fined or lose my licence. If I give you anything and it turns out you have internal injuries, well, you could die! I'm sorry, but you will have to see a doctor first, young fellow,' were the final words on the matter from the old chap.

Recognising that there was no way of getting around the man, Blackie lied once more, thanking the old bloke for his advice and assuring him that he would take himself to the hospital directly. As Blackie shuffled away, he cursed the old bastard and his friggin rules. Blackie felt like knocking all the goods – the stupid perfumes, the deodorants, the aftershave, the knick-knacks and hair dyes – from the shelves and send them sailing. He wanted to yell at the old man to go and fuck himself. But he kept his mouth shut and said nothing, making his way through the exit and out onto the footpath and into the fresh air.

He stood leaning against the wall on the corner, wondering what to do as he watched the rain. He looked across the road through the gloom into the park. He squinted to make out the form that he imagined he'd seen. There, huddled under the gum tree, were three dark figures. At first he thought of the three witches in the opening scene from *Macbeth.*

'*Where shall we three meet again? In thunder, lightning, or in rain?*' Blackie remembered from the play.

Blackie recalled the ghost's prophecy to the gullible 'would-be king'.

Be bloody, bold, and resolute. Laugh to scorn
The power of man, for none of woman born
Shall harm Macbeth.

'*So foul and fair a day I have not seen!*' Blackie whispered as he remembered more from Shakespeare's great tragedy.

He wondered what those three dark figures in the park might be planning, plotting or pledging to one another. His thoughts were interrupted when two of the three stepped from their shelter beneath the tree and began swinging punches at each other. Blackie watched as the two fighters traded hits while they slid and slipped in the mud. No witches were they, Blackie knew.

They were blackfullas.

They looked to be drunk, dressed like fringe dwellers or maybe street people, raggedy and dirty from living in the long grasses. Blackie knew the look. The rags, the desperation, the loneliness, the worn-out bags of bones. They slipped and slid on the wet ground, fighting to stand tall, fighting for space. No one but Blackie noticed. No one saw them get into it there, in the park. Blackie strained to hear their sad and angry voices, but their voices were lost to the howling wind and drowned by the pelting rain.

Watching the lonely scene reminded him of the night two years ago when he spied old Black Tom. Tom, drunk, but not defeated, standing there alone in the dark alleyway at the Cross. Black Tom, the homeless man who read an abridged version of Keats on the sidewalks of the Cross. The man who'd once worked as a lawyer in

Pitt Street, Sydney. Who had dined in blue suits at The Rocks. The same man who'd lost it all when he shot his wife when he found her in bed with his partner. Tom put the gun to his own head and pulled the trigger, the bullet grazed his brain and the court found him incapable to stand trial for her murder because of diminished responsibility.

Blackie remembered how the old man stood defiant in the pouring rain. Blackie saw Tom tear his shirt from his back, and shake his fists to the night sky, and scream to no one there – not even a chair, 'Why me?'

Blackie remembered the scene of police and ambulance officers as they gathered at Black Tom's wrecked body two days later when he was discovered dead on the overgrown block.

'Why me?' muttered Blackie, remembering. 'Why me?'

Remembering Tom, and remembering the scene in the chemist's shop, and remembering the behaviour of the white woman who at first refused to look at him, brought wildness back to Blackie's mind.

'Fuck whitefullas, the dogs,' he whispered. 'Why it always gotta be this way?' Blackie asked louder, to no one there.

Blackie shook his head sadly and refocused his thoughts back on the two men brawling in the park. They looked like they had both run out of puff and collapsed into each other's arms with apparently no real damage done to either one. They were brothers, once more. And once more were being held together in brothers' arms. He began scouring the park for any other signs of life that might be lingering there. He quickly stood to attention when he came across the shape of a woman, hanging there, alone in the weather.

'She not real!'

'She *can't be* real.'

'How can she be? Her feet don't touch the ground!'

He blinked to get a clearer picture. But when he opened his eyes, the vision was gone. He stood ramrod straight. He searched for her again. Where had the strange woman gone? He looked from tree to tree, but she wasn't there. His anxious search took him from the palms to the gums, from the shrubs to the bushes.

'Where'd ya fucken go?' he murmured. '*Fuck,* my eyes!'

His search was disrupted by the loud beeping of a car horn that drew him back to other people's presence. Rips and Tegan had arrived to collect him.

'Fuck ya, Rips!' he cursed softly.

The new lovers brought with them their urgency for Blackie to hurry so they could be gone to do their sexy business again. It forced him to move towards the car and it left him feeling completely unfulfilled and yearning. Tegan told Blackie where he could buy plastic boomerangs for the twins, and upon purchasing them, Blackie decided to get something for Dot, Fingers, Silvia and Silvia's baby as well. Blackie, Rips and Tegan fished around the mall peering through the shop windows until Rips spotted a wheelchair that was available for the disabled. Big Rips was quick to pounce. He returned to Blackie and Tegan with a mad smile a mile wide across his face, pushing the bright orange-flagged chair for Blackie to use.

''Ere Black. Sit ya black arse in dere, man. Git round in style brother! Fuck the Gubbas! They not the only ones thas loud ta use these things, man. You crook man!'

They erupted into loud, uncontrollable laughter, and despite Rips' crazy request, Blackie played along, sliding into the chair. Rips pushed off before he was completely settled safely, forcing the chair into a wheelie, with Blackie gripping hard and cursing along the way.

13

A Twist for the Twisted

The car ride back to Dot and Fingers' place was a fast one. Tegan was driving fast trying to race the wind through the deserted streets. Carefree and all messed up in love, she'd never felt so much freedom and joy as she did in her little Toyota Corolla. She drove the fast car through the wind and the rain with the greatest of ease, while Rips played with her thigh, tickling to tease.

On the back seat, surrounded by gifts, Blackie finally began to feel good about everything. The pain in his gut had eased and was almost gone, bringing with it sweet relief. And the speed he'd taken had him feeling like he was flying. He felt happier than he had in a very long while. He breathed a deep sigh of satisfaction, closed his eyes, and smiled. The worries that had brought him into the storms of life had, temporarily at least, flown away.

Rips began singing 'Hey, Good Lookin''. He sang all the way to Dot's house.

*

With hearts filled with gladness and arms full with food and gifts falling from their grasp and spilling around them, they stumbled up the steps and onto the rain-soaked porch, giggling like kids do when they've done something wrong or silly. They almost fell into the living room as they squeezed through the doorway. But the scene that was set before them as they stepped into the silent room filled their hearts with fear and dread.

The twins were clinging to the side of their mother's dress, their little faces buried deep into their mumma's side. Dot stood there stiff as if in shock with her eyes tearing, leaving her with a stained face. The tears rolled away and got lost in the wrinkles on her face, spreading sideways and disappearing away across her cheeks. Dot's other two boys, Kiah and Patrick, now home, sat with their arms folded as tight as closed envelopes on the lounge. Glum-faced with downcast eyes, Kiah and Patty appeared as though they'd been crying also. They gave Blackie a quick glance of acknowledgement with a nod of their heads, and then turned away, doing their best to hold back their tears and anger. Blackie threw his gifts to the empty lounge chair and rushed to his cousin, Dot.

'What 'appened, cuz? Who died?' he asked wildly.

'Oh, Black! Coppers come and took Fingers! They're lookin for you and Rips,' Dot answered with a slow shake of her head.

'What? What for? What they pinch Fingers for?' Blackie questioned.

'Said you fullas stole a car last night, or somethin. Whatcha's do, Black?' Dot asked.

Blackie looked at Rips, who, in turn, looked away in shame, and was no help. Needing time to think, Blackie said, ''Ere. Come and sit down, cuz.'

Although he was feeling rage and hatred for the coppers surging through his body, he held himself together tightly. He began to consider what to do to resolve the mess he'd caused everybody. He did his best to help his stunned cousin, by the offer of his arm, to the empty lounge chair. She gathered up the twins and nursed them safely in her arms. Blackie was pleased when Silvia appeared from the kitchen with yet another tray of cups filled with hot tea. She looks as hot as the tea, he thought. Funny he hadn't recognised that she was so pretty, so elegant, before. She caught him looking at her, and embarrassed, they both looked away from each other in a flash. Blackie got his mind back to the business. He kept turning over the situation, feeling responsible and terrible. He thought there and then that his nan had been trying to warn him all along to stay away. That's why she hadn't left him alone! That's why he smelt her scent.

He knew that the storm was a sign of bad things to come.

That the wind was his warning for him to blow out of town.

That the apparition in the graveyard yesterday afternoon, and the floating woman in the park, were warning him of the dangers he had brought to Dot and to her family.

That the men fighting in the park had warned him of the fight he now found himself in.

But did he listen to the wind?

No!

Did he understand the storm?

No!

Did he read the signs?

No! No, No, No fucken NO!

'Some fucken blackfulla I am!'

Feeling that his fate was cast like that of Macbeth, he decided that, like Macbeth, he'd take whatever came his way, best he could. Now came time for him to pay the price for every bloody thing he'd done.

If only he hadn't been so bloody busy being a big man – looking for drugs, wanting to drink, looking for fights, maybe these things would not have happened. Oh, why hadn't he taken more notice of the ghost in the cemetery? He didn't heed the warnings. He cursed himself for being so blind to that other world. He understood now what a shitty situation he'd brought down upon his relations and friends.

And he knew he had to fix it. He remembered the wind pushing him forwards and backwards and to the west in the cemetery. Finally, he understood. Well, he thought he did anyway.

Poor Blackie! One of his great gifts was that he was calm in a crisis. He was the sort of person that could automatically take charge at an accident scene. He wouldn't let fear hold him back. He was the kind of person others would look towards for advice and protection in such times as that. Blackie took command and controlled the pace of things, while giving himself time to consider.

'Fuck it. I'll be cool. Just gotta be calm,' he whispered. Thinking and hoping, Blackie tried to clear his mind. He was hoping to get this mess cleaned up as quickly as possible. And he was thinking of how to resolve it. He stirred the cup of hot tea and passed it to Dot. Silvia collected the twins, and took them into the kitchen for comfort food, and away from the grown-ups, while the grown-ups did their grown-up things.

'Now ... tell me again what happened. What'd the dogs say?' Blackie asked.

The pretty Tegan had her hair tied up in a black ribbon that hung down the middle of her back. She sat quietly with Rips, listening.

Dot's furrowed brow began to soften now that Blackie was back and giving her a hand. 'It's alright Blackie. Not your fault. These bastard cops always on our back here. They came about, oh ... a good hour ago I s'pose ... It's a wonder you didn't pass them on your way downtown. They got here soon after you left,' Dot said.

Blackie looked at Rips. Rips looked at Tegan and Tegan grabbed Rips' arm.

★

'Yeah. We passed 'em alright, ay Rips?' Blackie said.

Rips nodded.

'That bastard! Hunter McWilliams was the big shot, Black. Said something about another bloke. Carl or Carly, somefin like that? Know anything bout him?' Dot asked.

She obviously wanted Blackie or Rips to shed some light on the reason the police were after them, and as to why they'd taken her old man.

'McWilliams, hey?' Blackie asked.

A plan was beginning to take shape in his mind.

'Fucken Carlos!' Rips swore.

Blackie gave the shaky Dot a little hug of reassurance and said, 'It'll be right, cuz. I'll git him out. No worries.'

Despite the madness of the situation they found themselves in, Dot believed that somehow Blackie could do it. Even when he bullshitted her, it made her feel better. He just had that way about him that brought her both heartache and comfort. But she could always count on her cousin to be there when the chips were down, and when danger loomed in every place, Blackie'd be there to do what he could to help. Like how he turned up with cash from out of the blue and paid in full for her dad's funeral. Like the many times he'd be on hand when push came to shove and her boys were being bullied by cops or other thugs. Blackie'd jest smile and say, 'She'll be right, cuz. I take care of it.' And despite the odds, Blackie'd mostly come up trumps and set the problems to rights. Dot had tears in her eyes knowing that the cost of all these dramas was mostly borne by Blackie. And now what? What would this cost him? she thought.

''Ere, Rips. Help me up brother. Take me to the toilet, mate,' Blackie said.

Rips took Blackie's arm and Dot watched as Blackie gingerly walked across the lonely floor, into the hallway. She knew that there was something very wrong with him and it frightened her to her bones. She knew that she couldn't fix him up this time. Dot thought how bad luck and misery seemed to follow Blackie everywhere he went. So she told herself that she'd march straight down to that station, kids at her side, and free her man!

'You coppers ain't seen nothin yet!' she whispered.

In the bathroom, sweat was pouring out of both black men. Rips' eyes were big like fifty-cent pieces and the frown on his face told Blackie that his big mate was wild with worry.

'That fucken arsehole, Carlos!' Rips cursed. 'I, I, I'll fucken smash 'im w, w, when I see 'im!' he promised. 'I'll kill that bastard!'

'Yeah. Drive that little *cunt* when ya see him for me, brother,' Blackie said.

Blackie sat on the toilet seat as Rips positioned himself beside him on the edge of the bathtub. They figured that Carlos had been out showing off, driving black women around town, looking for what he'd fantasised about the night before, an easy fuck, and got pulled over by cops. Carlos would have given up Blackie and Rips faster than a snakebite. Rips and Blackie knew only too well what a weak-arse bastard Carlos was. Blackie grabbed for the towel and wiped his face dry, then handed it to Rips who did the same.

'Wa, wa, whatcha gonna do, Black? I ain't far, far, fucken goin back ta gaol, man!' Rips stuttered. Rips' voice showed the strain of worry and despair of a gaol proposition. Blackie knew another round in the clink would kill his old brother.

'Don't worry, bra. I know that McWilliams. It'll be right. You should piss off 'fore they come back, bud. Take Tegan with ya. They'll probably 'ave her name now, too. Git away from 'ere. Say g'day to ya mum for me, ay? Tell her I'll see her again soon, no worries, bud,' Blackie said, without much confidence.

Rips asked, 'Whatcha gonna do, Black?'

'Well, first of all, um gonna have another crack at dat Force ya got in ya pocket there, bra,' Blackie said, smiling.

Rips smiled back: he wanted more of the powerful speed too. Blackie knew well how the speed brought him comfort. It took him far away from the troubles of this world and into another one, where all things were possible and everything free and easy. It's a junkie's way, that way. A *real* highway to hell. Although both men were revved up from the drug they'd taken before, they dug in again. Blackie swore about the taste and almost vomited again. Rips laughed at him.

''Ere, Black. You take dis. I'll git some more on da way out,' Rips declared as he passed the remains of the bag of speed to Blackie.

Rips then drew from his pocket crisp, clean-smelling bank notes, tied up in a red rubber band. He withdrew from the bundle and kept just one hundred dollars, and then thrust the rest into Blackie's palm.

'What's this, big fulla?' Blackie asked, surprised.

Blackie attempted to give the money back, but Rips would hear none of it.

'Eight 'undred dere, cuz. You keep it, man. I still got eight thousand in da bank. Old Rips, right.'

As Blackie started to protest the gift, Rips waved his arm, blocking him before he had a chance to say anything about the money.

Blackie understood the gesture and just said, 'Okay. Ta, bud.'

They both washed and dried their faces, and shared their moment before returning to the lounge room. The pain had begun to return to Blackie's stomach and it made him double up as he walked. The twins had settled down and were once again sitting either side of their mother, staring at Blackie with big eyes. Understanding that their bravery was covering their fear brought deep pain to Blackie. He knew that no child should have to be traumatised by witnessing their father being snatched from them – especially on their birthday. The fact that this house had been turned upside down, and he was to blame, made him wild with himself. His anger gave him strength and his mind ruled over the physical pain he'd been feeling. The 'steel' in him let him know that given the chance, he'd be able to make a stand and take on anyone, there and then. He knew that 'true' strength found its life in love, and everything else was bullshit. And he loved this family as he did no other. Blackie decided that he'd do something to lighten the load they were all carrying.

'Hey, cuz?' he said to Dot. 'Reckon it'd be alright ta give these two big fullas their birthday present?' he said, with a smile. The boys sat straighter and smiles replaced their frowns.

'Yeah, course ya can!' Dot said happily.

Everyone gathered around and waited patiently as the twins took no time at all at tearing the paper wrapping clear to discover their gifts.

'AHHH! Unca Black,' said Vincent excitedly. 'Is we real abba, abba, *dig*inezes now?'

He held the boomerang tight in his grasp and struck a pose as if to let it rip. Ralph followed suit and the room erupted in laughter at the boys' attempt.

'You sure are, brother! You a real "Abadiginee" now, alright. You always a real one, big fulla,' Blackie assured.

'And you're what?' Dot asked with a smile.

'We're black and deadly! Yay!' the twins yelled.

'Don't you fullas chuck them in this house!' she roused, just as Ralph was about to try to take his brother's head off with a throw.

'Well, can we go outside and play then, Mum?' Vincent asked.

'What! You bloody mad or somethin? No! Ya bloody can't go outside! Ya wanna git blown away, hey? You'll end up in Timbuktu or somewhere!' Dot argued.

The blue gum tree in front of a neighbour, two doors down from Dot's place, had fallen and crushed a car on the street. The SES workers tussled with the wind and rain to cut the long branches and free the vehicle. The chainsaw was just audible above the wind.

Vincent had something else to say on the matter too, but Dot was ready for him and shut him down before he could get the words out.

'And before *you* say anything, Vince – the answer is still no!'

Vince blinked and his argument froze in his throat. He looked at his two older brothers, who giggled, and then he launched himself at them full tilt with a playful roar. The boys wrestled and tumbled onto the floor and fell on Dot's feet, squashing her sore toes.

'Git away you boys! I'll git up for you in a minute! Take 'em in the room there, you big boys!' she yelled.

When they reached the hallway, without speaking, the twins jointly spun on their heels, and flew back and wrapped their arms around Blackie's waist.

'Thanks Unca Blackie!' they said together, and then they were gone again.

Not being used to being around young children, the tender moment took Blackie by complete surprise and left him feeling happy and sad at the same time.

'Hey, look Dot,' Blackie said then. 'Coppers will

prob'ly be back, so these fullas gonna git goin,' he said, referring to Tegan and Rips.

'Yeah, that's a good idea. You know what they're like alright,' Dot said. Rips and Tegan kept their goodbyes to a minimum. Tegan cried. 'See ya, Aunty Dot,' she said. Dot kissed her cheek and said, 'You watch yaself, girl.'

Dot gave Rips a stern look and warned, 'You look after this girl, boy!' Rips looked down and nodded his head. The moment was a sad one for all as they faced their goodbye. Rips looked up and turned to Blackie and quietly said, 'Stay strong, bra! See ya.' He then turned and disappeared like a phantom out into the wind and the rain.

14

Give up, Give in

Blackie felt sorry seeing his big mate leave, but he knew it was the best thing in order to keep Rips safe … Silvia returned from a bedroom where she'd been nursing her Jimmy and sat holding Dot's hand.

Blackie finally broke the silence by saying, 'I know that McWilliams, he's from Bourke. He's me mate. I'll go down there and talk to him. I'll see if these whitefullas are fair dinkum bout this reconciliation shit! I'll give meself up! And den let's see if they'll let Fingers go. It's me dey want anyway, so, she'll be right.'

Dot said, 'That's not what reconciliation's all about Blackie. You can't do that!'

'Well, when dey all marched across the bridge down there in Sydney, I wuz on me way up ta see what the fuss wuz bout. They had "S-O-R-R-Y" written in the sky and ebreyding. Ya know what the bastards did ta me? Two pigs strip-searched me in the toilet in the park – jest cause I'm a blackfulla – jest cause dey could! Pulled a fucken gun on me and ebreyding, they did! I got nothin from reconciliation. Fuck 'em! They owe!' Blackie said.

Dot worried about what Blackie might do next. She sat quiet. But she could not think of a thing to do. She began to cry and her boys cried too.

'Fuck this,' Blackie said, standing and struggling with his sore stomach.

He reached Dot and put his arm on her shoulder.

'She'll be right, cuz,' he said. 'Here, you take this,' he said smiling, placing a fistful of the dollars that Rips had given him onto her lap. 'It's not much, but it might help ya a bit.'

Dot looked at Blackie, trying to thank him, but just nodded her head.

'Won't need it where um going, cuz,' Blackie assured.

Wiping her eyes with a stiff hanky, Dot complained, 'I can't let ya do that, Blackie!'

'She be right … I gotta dry out anyway. The rest'll do me good. She'll be right, Dot. No worries,' he answered.

The speed he'd swallowed was beginning to do its work. Grinding his teeth, sweat dripping down his neck, the shirt Fingers had lent him sticking to his back. He wiped his brow with the shirt sleeve and reached for his cold tea, took a swig and regretted doing so as it had turned bitter.

'Who's got a phone?' he asked. 'I'll git a cab down to the station.'

'I'll give ya a lift,' Silvia offered, a little too quickly.

She glanced towards Dot for some kind of approval. Dot nodded at her and reached to take little Jimmy.

'Okay. Ta,' Blackie said.

Blackie shook hands with the elder boys and wiped tears from his eyes as Dot cried at the door as she waved goodbye. She felt much pride in the fact that Blackie was so proud to be black. Proud too, that he would never give up, nor give in. She heard the car doors slam shut, and ached as she watched them drive out of the driveway and onto where Blackie's past and destiny would soon collide.

Silvia pulled the car to the side of the kerb a few feet from the police station. She looked at Blackie, and Blackie returned the gaze, both unsure what to do next.

He was sweating from the speed and sweating from what was coming next. He reached into his shirt pocket and drew from it the remainder of the cash. 'Here,' he said and placed the lot in Silvia's hand.

She sat shocked from his generosity. Before she said anything Blackie continued, 'See, sometimes dreams do come true. Wish I could do more for ya. Dunno if it's enough, but it might help ya ta git outa this "rathole" town as you call it ... I think Dubbo's a poxy place too!'

Silvia pressed into his arms and kissed him. The kiss was so sweet. Blackie eased away from her gently and said, 'Wish I had more time, but I gotta go.' He took a deep breath and took in all her smell. He liked it a lot. But that was his problem. If he allowed it, he'd probably end up liking her too much and he hated commitments that he would not keep and so, without another word spoken between them, he opened the door and left her there alone in the car.

'Hey, Blackie … Don't go yet,' Silvia called.

She opened the window and Blackie leant on the frame.

'Don't worry bout it,' he said. 'Tell ya what. How bout ya write ta me, ay? I like letters. I'm gonna be locked up for a while by the looks-a it. Dot's got me MIN number. Probably send me ta Silverwater for assessment first. Dunno where afta that though. Dot'll know, so jest ask her.'

Silvia said, 'Take care, Black. Take care …' and then cried.

'I'll be right. Look after that little fulla. Look after yaself too. See ya,' Blackie replied, and then turned to walk up the steps to the police station front door.

Walking hunched over with his head tucked onto the shoulder as he braced against the beautiful storm. At the doorway, he propped and turned and waved to her and watched as she drove away.

He suddenly felt very old. He stuck his tongue out to taste the rain.

'See ya, Dubbo. See ya, Mum. See ya, Nan. See ya all later,' he spoke to the sky.

15

Police Negotiation Ain't Negotiation at All

The cop shop was the same as all the rest he'd been through. Efficient was the word he'd used to describe them. Everything bolted down and made of steel. Blackie assumed it was so blackfullas like himself couldn't steal any of it. As if he'd want to, he mused. Missing people, illegal weapons and other similar posters adorned the dreary walls painted in cream and grey, warning the public of one thing or another. He was breathing hard when he straightened himself up, and made his way to the counter. On the other side, a young constable sat with head down, staring seriously at a computer screen. The sound of a distant dispatch being radioed to someone somewhere broke the silence. The reception area and the office were empty save for Blackie and the copper, and the whole scene had an air of loneliness about it. Blackie hoped he wouldn't live to regret what he was about to do. He smiled a cynical smile and prayed, 'Lord, please make me thankful for that which I am about to receive.'

The young police officer almost toppled from his

chair when he looked up to see the black man standing silently, staring.

'Hello. I didn't hear you come in,' he said in a cheerful manner. 'How can I help you?'

He rose from his chair and approached Blackie at the counter. He couldn't have been any more than twenty-one or -two. Blackie thought how stupid it was to give a man not long out of shorts a gun and a licence to use it. The pink face of the policeman, full of youth and cheeriness, seemed out of place to Blackie. The copper looked as though he would have better been suited to serving food at Macca's rather than to be in charge of the front desk at Dubbo Police Station. His bright face still had pimples left from his youth, his tender white skin showed that he'd been shaving for only a short while. Blackie noticed how the cop's yellow hair bounced as he walked. Thick and full was his hair, so unlike the scraggy mop that adorned Blackie's head.

'Ah, the beauty of youth,' Blackie sighed, 'so wasted on the young.' Blackie looked hard at the man in blue opposite him before he spoke.

'Yeah mate. I wanna see Hunter McWilliams,' Blackie said slowly.

'Sure,' said the constable. 'Who shall I say is calling, sir?' he asked politely.

'He knows me as Blackie. Jest let him know Blackie from Bourke's 'ere, ay?'

'Okie dokie. If you'd like to take a seat, I'll let him know you are here,' the young copper said.

Blackie watched as the man turned and walked back to his desk, picked up a telephone, and made the call to the big boss upstairs. Blackie knew that the shit would hit the fan as soon as McWilliams heard mention of his name and so sat with his hands in plain view, waiting for the expected to arrive. And, as expected, at the mention of his name, the police officers sprang into action. The side door flew open and two coppers with revolvers drawn burst through screaming at Blackie.

'Hands behind your head! Hands behind your head!'

More officers arrived into the lobby with revolvers drawn.

'So much overkill,' Blackie groaned.

The first policeman that had burst through the doorway manhandled Blackie to the ground, driving his knee into Blackie's back, and snapped handcuffs on so tight that Blackie thought he'd broken his wrist. Another pushed his face into the floor. Like a struggling calf that had just been bulldogged to the ground, Blackie was left struggling for wind. He pulled a half-arsed smile, showing the cops that they couldn't break his spirit, no matter how hard they tried. His wish was that all this crap would soon be over and done with.

'Cunts! Ya fucken white cunts!' he spat as he tried to turn his face from the dirty floor.

The police officers said nothing. Smug with their capture, they all waited with bated breath for their big chief to arrive. They didn't have to wait long. McWilliams walked into the waiting room, so vain and so full of shit, just like he was walking onto a yacht. Blackie could not see McWilliams' pomp and pride as his face was hard pressed against the lino floor. Blackie spat dirt and blood onto the floor which bounced back and splattered on his own face. He strained to look out from under the grasp of the police officers, only to see spit-polished shiny shoes. The shoes belonging to McWilliams.

McWilliams said, 'Get him up.'

The other policemen roughed Blackie up – pulling him, pushing down again, and pulling him up again, as they dragged Blackie to his feet. Blackie pushed with all his strength, trying to force the police to fall. They tussled with each other in a violent struggle. Blackie spat blood at the dogs who handled him so violently, only to be punched in the mouth and to fall to the ground again.

'Git the bastard up!' McWilliams yelled.

Blackie was all done when they pulled him to his feet again. No fight left in him this time. He leant heavily on his captors.

McWilliams had clenched fists and was about to let them fly into Blackie, but decided against it when he saw that Blackie was fucked.

Catching his breath, Blackie watched a policeman run a metal detector over his clothes. Blackie was thankful that he'd left his little pocket knife with Rips as they shook hands at Dot's place.

'He's clean, Boss,' he announced.

Blackie stood dribbly in front of McWilliams. Blackie focused on Red-Face's eyes, and forced a half-smile, trying to defy McWilliams. McWilliams smiled that ugly big grin he showed Blackie in court the day they locked Blackie away. He big-noted himself in front of his men, puffing his chest out, appearing even bigger than he was.

'Ahh, me old "mate", Blackie!' McWilliams sneered. 'Got you at last!'

The other police followed suit and swelled out their chests too. They stood with fierce stares with hands on their hips, standing close enough to Blackie so he could smell their stinking cop breaths.

Blackie's top lip, nose and the cut above his eyebrow (patched by Dot) now had blood flowing freely. But his adrenaline had kicked in and, apart from the handcuffs, he hardly felt a thing. He thought how he'd like to bust the bastard who drove his knee into his back. The bastard who now stood beside him, looking like a trained mutt waiting to be praised by its master with a pat on the head for a deed well done. Police had lit a fire in the black man's soul many moons ago. Blackie knew he'd never want to light candles in the rain or ever live as brothers with them. But Blackie decided to keep his powder dry. He was here to get Fingers out, so he had to shut his mouth for the time being and allow the pigs to have their fifteen minutes of fame.

McWilliams ordered Blackie to be taken to an empty interview room where he was left seated on the hard chair at the hard table.

Slow minutes ticked by and still his blood, made thin from the speed he'd taken, flowed freely from his wounds. The sticky blood ran down his hot face and fell onto his jeans which were becoming soaked from it. Blackie's eye was so swollen that, along with the blood flow, it made it impossible for him to see. His stomach was tight. Though he'd not eaten a thing in almost three days, his gut was full. He knew at that moment, that it wasn't a shit that he needed to take, that would put everything back on the even. He didn't know what was wrong but he knew that something was.

The heavy door swung open and in walked McWilliams – coffee in one hand, notepaper in the other – still full of shit.

McWilliams had been waiting to get Blackie alone again so he could deal with him once and for all. 'No getting outa gaol again this time, you little black bastard,' he said as he slumped in his chair.

McWilliams was a highly decorated police officer. Medals for service and medals for bravery adorned the wall above his desk. But behind the scenes he slept with some black women, and shared a bottle or two with some black men. It was true enough. McWilliams wasn't all bad. But he was corrupt. And he could as easily show kindness, if it benefited him, as he could be hard and mean.

McWilliams threw the paperwork on the desk and said, 'You really think you could beat *me*, Blackie? I crush maggots like you.'

'How bout takin these cuffs off then, and we'll see

who fucken crushes who!' Blackie yelled.

'Now settle down there, old mate … Or I might have to get rough with you,' McWilliams said.

Blackie sat as straight as his stomach allowed and said nothing.

McWilliams watched Blackie and then smiled at him. 'Good. That's better. Now we can talk,' McWilliams declared.

After another minute of flicking through the pages of Blackie's file the policeman said, 'Well, Blackie. Long time no see, hey? You've been busy. Very busy bastard, haven't you?'

Blackie did his best to laugh it off.

'Ahh. You know how it is? … Long time no see, alright,' Blackie acknowledged.

'Well you're in a lota trouble, my friend!' McWilliams declared.

'What! Over a fucken stolen car! Don't think so mate,' Blackie returned serve.

The mind games had begun. Attack and counterattack. McWilliams tried to ignore Blackie's remark by casually taking a loud slurp from his coffee. 'Ahh! Gee that's bloody good!' he said, winking, hoping to get a rise out of Blackie.

Blackie was very thirsty, and the sight of the coffee made him lick his dry lips, only to taste his own blood.

'Now let's see what we've got here,' McWilliams said.

The policeman pretended to study Blackie's 'form' with all the interest a punter does with the race guide on

Cup Day. McWilliams whistled something and slowly turned the pages. Occasionally he'd turn back to check something in the papers, dragging the whole affair out, making Blackie suffer in waiting. Blackie shifted side to side on the chair. His shirt stuck to his back and his skin began to itch. Oh how he wished he could be free just to have a good scratch. Blackie tried to amuse himself by humming the Talking Heads song 'Once in a Lifetime'.

Eventually McWilliams became bored with his pretence and placed the papers to the side. He leant back in his chair, folded his arms and sighed loudly. Blackie sat straight and attentive, the perfect foil. Where both men came together was that they both enjoyed playing the game.

'Got something you wanna tell me, Blackie? Anything I should know, hey?' McWilliams said with a half-smile.

'Yeah I 'ave as matter-a fact,' Blackie replied softly. 'You got a mate of mine 'ere. He's me brother-in-law. He's got nuffin to do with all-a dis. Let him go and I'll tell ya what ya wanna hear. It's his kids' birthday, man!' Blackie pleaded.

'Well! We'll just have to see about that now, won't we? He's facing very serious charges. What do I get outa this, huh?' McWilliams said, now very interested in what was beginning to sound like a policeman's jackpot: a confession.

Blackie thought about his next move very carefully before he said, 'Got anyone for that thing back 'ome?' referring to the attack on the police station in Bourke.

Big McWilliams revelled in his victory.

'Yeah … I got you, babe!' he mocked.

Blackie looked at the ugly man carefully, fully expecting a backhander for what he was about to say, but spoke bravely anyway. 'You got jack shit man! I wasn't even in town. But I think I know who did it, but thas another story. You let Fingers go, and then we'll talk, man ta man.'

That took a bit of the wind out of the copper's sails, but McWilliams knew he had Blackie between a rock and a hard place.

McWilliams said, 'Remember how all your blacks would rush to watch ya run? Watch ya play footy? Yeah? Well where are they now, huh? And you still trying to be their hero aren't ya? Play this right, Blackie, and your brother will walk. But if you don't give me what I want, you're both fucked. Okay?'

Blackie nodded.

McWilliams leant closer and told Blackie, in whispers, that nothing more than a full confession from him would have Fingers released, and that would be that. The stakes had suddenly jumped very high. The time for games was over. This was real serious stuff that the men were playing with.

McWilliams knew that nothing short of an airtight and full confession admitting total responsibility for the firebombing (almost seven years ago) on the station would put Blackie away for life, regardless of the truth. Blackie would never be able to be taken seriously by any court again. As such, McWilliams' 'deal' with Blackie would remain a secret to the grave. He'd have his promotion and power, but equal to that, he'd finally be able to say that he'd beaten the black man for good.

Blackie's gain would be that his family would be safe. Fingers, he knew, was a good and decent man that would lay his life down for Dot and the kids. That'd be enough for Blackie to give what he could to make it square. He knew that someone had to pay for the stolen car and his wild ways. And that person was going to be Blackie himself.

Suddenly, and without warning, Blackie vomited all over the table. His spew soaked the notes that McWilliams had brought in with him, and narrowly missed the policeman.

'What the fuck! You dirty, black *bastard*!' McWilliams cursed. 'Look whatcha fucken done!'

But Blackie was too crook to be concerned with any more games. He rested his head on his arm on the table and closed his eyes.

'Sorry, bra. Musta been somefin in the water.'

Although Blackie felt bad, the vomiting made him feel a bit better.

McWilliams left the room without another word as Blackie rested at the stinking table.

The young polite man who had greeted Blackie

earlier entered the room wearing rubber gloves and a face mask, carrying a mop and bucket with industrial-strength bleach.

The policeman looked at Blackie for a long while, looking for signs of life. He saw Blackie's breath and then asked, 'You alright there, mate?'

Blackie lifted his head, and nodded. 'Tell ya what, bra … How bout gittin us a drinka water, ay?'

The policeman placed his gear near the door, way out of Blackie's reach, and left. He quickly returned with a jug filled with cold water and a plastic cup. He placed them on the table and quietly went about the foul task of cleaning the vomit from table and floor.

'Ahh. Thanks, bud,' Blackie said as he sipped the cold drink.

The policeman said nothing, and when he finished the clean-up, he left, and Blackie was alone again. A good half-hour passed before Blackie heard the door latch turn and in walked McWilliams with Fingers. McWilliams directed Fingers to the table and told him to sit. Blackie did his best to appear brave in front of Fingers, but he found it very difficult to look good, smelling of spew.

'Now! Here's the plan, you bastards. You get one chance at this, and *one* chance only. *Hear*?' McWilliams said.

Blackie nodded.

'I'll leave your mate here with you for five minutes, you work out what you're gonna give me, and if it's right, he can go. But if you're fucken with me, there'll be no more mister nice guy, you black cunt. You'll both wish you weren't born! … *Five* minutes!' McWilliams screeched, slamming the door shut on his way out.

Blackie assured Fingers that he was alright. But any fool could see that he wasn't. His eyes were glassy, his black skin turned pale, and his lips were cracked and dry. All signs that Blackie was suffering badly. But still, he assured Fingers that he was alright.

'Um sweet, bra. They charge ya with anything?' he said softly.

'Naa. Jest had me sittin downstairs by meself! S'pose they were hopin ta git you and Rips,' Fingers answered.

'Well they got me, but they won't git Rips – he's long gorn. You git outa 'ere too when *he* comes back, bra. Git outa dis shithouse town, man. They don't like blackfullas here. Your two eldest boys are at the right age ta run inta trouble. And they're still lookin for Rips, so they be all over you, brother. Pack Dot and the kids up and git outa here, man,' Blackie whispered.

Fingers knew the truth in the words sure enough. Now that the cops had him in their sights, they'd hassle and harass him and his family at will. Fingers also knew that it would be the kids that would be the most vulnerable and susceptible to the cops' callous behaviour.

⋆

'Um worried bout Dot, mate. She don't look good ta me. She right brother, or what?' Blackie inquired.

Worried, Fingers said, 'Na, she's crook, Black. Diabetes got her fucked. Some days …' Fingers' voice trailed off, he choked back a sob.

Resting against each other in their chairs, Blackie leant his head on Fingers' shoulder. 'Git her away from here, mate. McWilliams will come afta her … And your boys too. Cause the bastards gonna put me away for good this time and Dot knows the truth. She knows that I was at old JK's place laid up with the flu when that shit in Bourke went down. I didn't blow up the police station, but they all reckon I did because they know I hate this cunt 'ere – McWilliams. He was stationed there then,' Blackie said, nodding towards the door – towards McWilliams.

'Git 'em to New Zealand bro, and don't come back,' Blackie whispered.

Fingers couldn't help it, he cried like a child – so broken-hearted.

'Ahh Blackie … Ya right, Black … Bet we broke. We're stuck here, mate,' Fingers replied.

'What bout ya people in New Zealand, man? Can't they help ya?' Blackie questioned.

'Dunno. I'll try. Whatcha think they'll do to you, Black?' Fingers asked, scared.

'She'll be sweet, man … prob'ly send me to Silverwater

for assessment. Don't worry, bruz, the change is gonna do me good,' Blackie said, smiling.

As Fingers nodded, the locked door swung open. McWilliams strode to the interview table and sat heavily on the other empty chair.

'Well?' he asked.

Blackie knew that he meant, 'Do we have a deal? Will you confess to a charge of terror attack upon a public building?'

Blackie didn't look up, just nodded and wished that he could drop dead on the spot.

Fingers looked away, not wanting to be witness to any of that business.

'Alright then!' said McWilliams, slapping the table apparently in joy and with great gusto.

'*You* come with me,' he said to Fingers.

'And I'll be back for *you* in a minute,' he said to Blackie.

McWilliams took Fingers back to the holding room. He wasn't going to let him go before he had Blackie's confession safe and secure on video.

The deal was that Blackie would nod his head for a petrol bomb attack on the Bourke Police Station. His most serious charges would be:

Riotous assault.

Assault of police.

Assault with a deadly weapon.

Using a telephone to menace.

Stealing a motor vehicle.

Evading apprehension.

Et cetera, et cetera, et-fucking-cetera …

McWilliams looked to Blackie that he was as happy as a pig in shit.

'Fuck ya, you dog. I'd never even piss on you if you was on fire,' Blackie said to himself as he watched McWilliams outa his one good eye.

All the charges, save the stealing a motor vehicle, were bodgie. Both cop and crim knew it, but no one else knew it, and that's what mattered most to McWilliams. Blackie was tired and wanted to lie down. He wanted to be away from where all the bright lights shone. He wanted to be in a quiet cell, alone and resting. McWilliams finally offered Blackie a coffee which Blackie accepted graciously.

'Finished at last!' McWilliams said, letting out a long breath. 'Have ya in a cell in a minute, Blackie.'

Blackie was not amused with McWilliams' change in mood and attitude towards him. Blackie knew that McWilliams had what he wanted and that was all there was to it. Had Blackie played hardball, then the 'interview' and 'negotiations' would have gone on and bloody on, well into the night and early morning. Blackie just didn't give a shit anymore.

McWilliams was true to his word though. He brought

Fingers back to Blackie to say goodbye, and had Blackie uncuffed and resting in a quiet cell alone within the hour.

The cell was just as dingy as cells could be – steel walls surrounded Blackie. There was a steel basin and sink, a bunk made of steel, no mattress, no blanket, no pillow. Just scratches on the walls – the word 'Judy' was etched on the steel wall. 'Judy' was framed inside a crude-looking love heart, a memory to a someone from an unknown prisoner that once spent time in the very place Blackie now found himself.

No longer was Blackie a 'person of interest'. All the police procedures went out the window with Blackie's arrest and charges. There was no phone afforded him. No contact made with the Aboriginal Legal Service. No Aboriginal police liaison officer available. No medical assessment or treatment offered. No watch was kept on him in his lonely prison cell. Blackie was just another black crim locked up, and society would be able to sleep easily again.

But Blackie was glad at last to be alone. He could just hear the rain on the roof above the sound of the air conditioner.

McWilliams told him that a truck would arrive as soon as he could arrange it and transport him to Wellington Correctional Centre for the night, and then he'd be off to Silverwater in the morning. Blackie just nodded, and that was the last he saw of his captor.

Blackie rolled on his side on the little bed and faced the wall. He still had something up his sleeve – literally. Taped to the inside of his left arm was almost two grams of high-quality speed and some cocaine that Rips had given him. Blackie was right when he assumed that the police wouldn't bother to remove the surgical tape from his arm. He was right when he assumed that they'd be more interested in checking him for weapons than to do a proper 'pat-down'.

Blackie thought of his old mate Crusoe as he swallowed the lot. He got up to gulp down water from the tap at the basin. In a short minute, the coke made him feel like he'd never felt before. Looking into the polished steel wall, Blackie could just make out his reflection, dulled, but visible still. He had to look hard, but his reflection was there, staring back out from the gaolhouse wall at him.

'Everything's softer ... better now, thank God,' he said.

The coming of evening brought for Blackie a clearer high. His rush was faster than usual. He was flying within a couple of minutes. He felt strangely relaxed. He felt alright. He splashed his face with water. The cold water refreshed him, as if giving him a new pair of eyes. He spoke to the face staring back.

'Ahh! Fuck that feels good. Goin downtown tonight, man.'

'Look in da mirror, bra. Bet I can't see me.'

'No?'

'It's the other me. Other me has taken me place! I'm the other me?'

'Hmm?'

'G'day, you cunt!' the 'other' him said.

He kept staring. Listened hard. But the bloody air conditioner and the noise in his head made it impossible to be sure, to be certain, what he thought the reflection said. The face was beginning to fade. Blackie rubbed the steel with his shirt sleeve to make it shine. He spat at the wall. He cleaned the spit with his shirt. It was only after that, that the spit-polished steel revealed the image he was looking for.

'Ahh … there you are,' Blackie whispered. 'Welcome back, brother.'

The reflection kept fading in and out of focus. He wiped his eyes to clear them. He heard the reflected face say to him, 'Yeah! Ahh yeah! Good to be fucken back!'

Blackie spun on his heels like Michael Jackson when he danced, and said aloud to the room that had suddenly turned to black:

'Yeah! Good to be fucken back.'

Blackie lay down.

He wondered where Rips was, and what he was doing.

He missed Dot, and smiled when he thought of the magic moment when he first saw Vince and Rrrrralllph.

In his mind, he saw the face of his old nan smiling at him; her arms held open, welcoming him. The ghost image of his grandmother was a moody shade of grey. The only colour of her beside that grey, was her jet-black eyes. In the darkened cell, her eyes shone more than any light in the interview room where Blackie had signed his life away. They were brighter than the twin boys' smiles. Her eyes were pure love. Blackie reached for her and closed his eyes. None of his injuries bothered him then. He didn't feel a thing.

He was glad he'd come to Dubbo after all.

Outside, the storm raged ... The wind howled around the corners of the police station. It battered and sandblasted the building as if trying to free Blackie by knocking the station down. Rain spat stinging little drops at the door, the roof, the whole bloody thing. Mother Nature hadn't forgotten her black son being held in custody. She was throwing her disgust at the dirty deeds done by the dirty policeman, with all the fury of a mother's love when her boys are being harmed. The wind howled louder, and all the lights went out for the town.

16

Leave It to the Wind

Rips hummed a tune as he rubbed Tegan's leg as he and Tegan drove on towards Coonamble. Rips figured that coppers would be watching his mother's place for him to arrive back in Walgett and said, 'Better we go this way to my brother's place in Coonamble and stay there for a while.'

Tegan nodded in agreement and through the storm they went. The rain pelted the little car, and the window-wipers were doing their best to clear a view.

'Fuck this storm, babe!' Rips cursed.

A bright flash lit up the world about a mile farther down the road.

'Pull up! Pull up, quick!' he yelled.

Tegan stopped the car at the side of the road, near the tree.

He got out and walked to the back of the car. The rain eased, and then stopped completely. The world went very quiet for a few moments, like they were in the eye of a storm.

Walking towards the burnt tree, Rips felt the wind

start up again, turning everything icy cold. Cold, like death. It shook Rips as he stood there, transfixed, staring at the charred trunk. He didn't even hear Tegan slam the car door or approach him. He just stood there.

Tegan looked at him and asked, 'What's the matter?'

'Blackie's gorn!' Big Rips said.

'Whatcha mean? How ya know that?' she asked.

'Said he'd show me when it happened. He's in the tree. Thas why the white gum's all black. It's Blackie,' Rips said.

Tegan was shocked, because she believed what Rips said to be true. She knew Blackie had a special kind of magic, but this kind of thing, she thought, was just old Dreamtime stories that her mother used to tell her and the other kids when she was younger. No one really believed them anymore, did they? They were just stories to frighten kids to sleep, to warn them not to go wandering around where wild things are. But here she stood, shocked by the magic. She didn't notice that tears streamed down her face. She didn't feel them. She just stood there holding on.

Rips fished from his pocket an eight ball of the Force. He dipped his finger right in until it reached the bottom. Satisfied with his finger being completely coated with the 'gas', he broke from Tegan and walked the entire distance around the trunk of the tree, rubbing speed into every nook and cranny he found.

'There, bra!' was all he spoke.

He took a long last look at the tree. He was happy thinking that his warrior mate was no longer in chains … that Blackie's spirit soared with the wind. That he was free.

As free as the fucken wind …

FIRST NATIONS CLASSICS

Bitin' Back by Vivienne Cleven
Introduction by Melissa Lucashenko

When the Blackouts' star player Nevil Dooley wakes one morning to don a frock and 'eyeshada', his mother's idle days at the bingo hall are gone forever. Mystified and clueless, single parent Mavis takes to bush-cunning and fast footwork to unravel the mystery behind this sudden change of face.

Funny and cleverly covert, too, this is a truthful rendering of small-town prejudice and racist attitudes. Hilarity prevails while desperation builds in the race to save Nevil from the savage consequences of his discovery in a town where a career in footy is a young black man's only escape. Neither pig shoots, bust-ups at the Two Dogs, bare-knuckle sessions in the shed nor even a police siege can slow the countdown on this human timebomb.

'The novel nimbly blends rollicking humour with gender issues and the realities of small town prejudice and racial intolerance.' **Tara June Winch**

ISBN 978 0 7022 6851 9

FIRST NATIONS CLASSICS

Smoke Encrypted Whispers
by Samuel Wagan Watson
Introduction by Tony Birch

Smoke Encrypted Whispers showcases Samuel Wagan Watson's imaginative brilliance and exceptional poetic skills. In this book, which also includes work from three previous collections, his poems pulse with the language and images of a mangrove-lined river city, the beckoning highway, the just-glimpsed muse, the tug of childhood and restless ancestors.

Wagan Watson's poetry is the work of an artist who speaks to a sense of our common humanity, and to a communal attachment to place. Reading this book is, as Tony Birch points out, 'like witnessing Bruce Springsteen meet the Dreamtime'.

'Sharp, urban and brilliant.' *The Age*

'Some of the most interesting, provocative and engaging prose around. He's made the prose poem his own.' *The Weekend Australian*

ISBN 978 0 7022 6857 1